THE RAVINE

THE RAVINE

A novel of suspense by

Phyllis Brett Young

A
Ricochet
Book

Véhicule Press

Published with the generous assistance of the Canada Council
for the Arts and the Canada Book Fund of the Department
of Canadian Heritage.

Canada Council   Conseil des arts
for the Arts   du Canada

Canadä

Series editor: Brian Busby
Adaptation of original cover: J.W. Stewart
Special assistance: Willow Little
Typeset in Minion and Bernard Condensed
by Simon Garamond
Printed by Livres Rapido Books

LIBRARY AND ARCHIVES CANADA CATALOGUING IN PUBLICATION

Title: The ravine / by Phyllis Brett Young ; introduction by Amy
Lavender Harris.
Names: Young, Phyllis Brett, author. | Harris, Amy Lavender,
1972- writer of introduction.
Description: Series statement: A Ricochet Book | Originally
published under author's pseudonym of
Kendal Young : Toronto : Longman's, ©1962.
Identifiers: Canadiana (print) 20190235888 | Canadiana (ebook)
20190235896 | ISBN 9781550655445
(softcover) | ISBN 9781550655506 (HTML)
Classification: LCC PS8547.O58 R3 2020 | DDC c813/.54—dc23

Published by Véhicule Press, Montréal, Québec, Canada
www.vehiculepress.com

Distribution in Canada by LitDistCo
www.litdistco.ca

Distribution in the U.S. by Independent Publishers Group
www.ipgbook.com

Printed in Canada on FSC certified paper

INTRODUCTION

Amy Lavender Harris

Can a place be evil? Can a location—a building, a cross-roads, a ravine—be imbued with so much inherent malevolence that it draws out the most depraved of human impulses, including the urge to rape, defile, and kill? Or are 'bad' places merely projections of the darkness we are loathe to admit lies within us, a darkness drawn to locations where, under the cover of isolation or twilight, it may enact its lascivious horrors?

Originally published in 1962, when psychological concepts revolving around neuroses and anxieties—particularly bodily ones—had entered the public lexicon, *The Ravine* is a darkly voyeuristic novel told with a psychoanalytic twist. The titular ravine is a geological anomaly: located at the geographical centre of an unnamed town, the ravine is a steeply sloped gully that has no natural drainage, has never been a watercourse, and is little more than a visible gash in the earth's fabric. No birds sing in the ravine; its trees are oddly stunted and seem to twist strangely in the wind. Even on a bright day the ravine remains deep in shadow, and a disquieting mist settles upon it at twilight. Few people enter the ravine: the only signs of their passage are furtive footpaths cutting across its boggy terrain.

Amid this climate of avoidance and fear, the ravine has exacted a toll on the town. A young girl is raped in its dank recesses and left brutalized and witless. The police mount an investigation but uncover few leads. The townspeople are disquieted but their concern seems oddly reticent. A local newspaper champions the ravine's destruction, mainly in a bid to increase circulation, but fails to drum up much popular support. The town is galvanized into action only when a second child is taken and discovered dead at the bottom of the ravine, her red raincoat spread around her like a pool of blood.

But even after this event the latest victim's discoverer, a young woman who has moved recently to town to teach art at the local primary school, is not believed when she describes the assailant whose face she has glimpsed briefly in the shadows. Her testimony at the public inquest—that the assailant had looked like the Devil himself—is met with derision and laughter. Only one man, a surgeon at the local hospital, believes her, because he alone knows someone, a sinuous man with a Gothic countenance, seemingly unimpeachable in profession and cloaked in the sheen of social respectability, who has both the aptitude and opportunity to slip unnoticed into the ravine in pursuit of his darkest and most destructive desires—and who, upon realizing that the young artist is a gifted illustrator with a photographic memory, will undoubtedly move to kill her before she can identify him. This tense realization propels the novel toward its culminating violence.

The novel's setting (an unnamed New England town divided topographically as well as socially by the ravine's sinister landscape), its protagonists (the pretty, blonde art teacher; the outwardly respectable but inwardly satanic predator who stalks and violates young girls; the perceptive doctor who acts on his suspicions; the brooding yet compassionate police investigator; the cynical newspaperman), and spare, tense, moralistic language would be familiar to midcentury readers of stories serialized in women's magazines. These qualities undoubtedly contributed to the novel's success—and perhaps its subsequent decline. Published in Canada and the UK in hardcover editions in 1962, followed by two paperback editions (1964; 1971), and in translation in Germany as *Mein Mörder kommt um 8* (*My Murderer Comes at 8*, 1966), the novel was subsequently adapted to the screen as a titillating thriller (*Assault*, 1971; later repackaged for television and VHS viewing under a variety of titles, among them *In the Devil's Garden*, *The Creepers*, and *Satan's Playthings*). After these releases the novel faded from view, much like its pseudonymous author, "Kendal Young." Is *The Ravine*, then, a nostalgia read? Not necessarily.

Six decades after its publication, *The Ravine* remains relevant reading. In the first instance, it brings renewed attention to the work of Phyllis Brett Young, a Canadian novelist of the midcentury known for her international bestsellers *Psyche* (1959) and *The Torontonians* (1960). When these long out-of-print novels were reissued (McGill-Queen's University Press, 2007 and 2008 respectively), attention focused mainly on Young's contributions to modernism in Canadian literature. But lurking behind Young's mannered prose and midcentury protagonists is a thematic link among her novels that has gone mainly overlooked: that apart from suburban satire of *The Torontonians* and a fictionalized memoir (*Anything Could Happen*, 1961), each of her novels employs the tropes of Gothic thrillers, featuring girls and young women variously stalked, abducted and assaulted or murdered by personages including an avaricious electrician (*Psyche*, 1959),the deviant doctor in *The Ravine*, the ghost of a new husband's dead wife (*Undine*, 1964), and a jealous lover (*A Question of Judgment*, 1969). Although published under a pseudonym meant to distinguish the novel from her other books, *The Ravine* actually has a great deal in common with Young's body of work—and with the evolving themes of Gothic, crime, and horror fiction published during the twentieth century. Perhaps most notably, in rewriting the tired tropes of sexual violence in ways that emphasize her female protagonists' agency, Young's work highlights problems of representation as relevant in the #metoo era as they were during the tumultuous 1960s.

Similarly, the psychospatial focus on the ravine—that "tangled, cancerous growth" at the centre of the town— puts Young in the company of other writers, perhaps most notable among them Margaret Atwood and Ray Bradbury, whose work also depicts ravines as sites of molestation and murder. Atwood places vulnerable young girls in harm's way in overgrown ravines in *Lady Oracle* (1976) and *Cat's Eye* (1988); in Bradbury's story "The Whole Town's Sleeping" (1950; the narrative also appears in his novel-in-stories *Dandelion Wine*, 1957), a spinster named Lavinia feels compelled to walk into a ravine, seething with midnight sounds, where three women have recently been raped and strangled. But where Atwood and Bradbury are content with ravines as sinister settings, in *The Ravine* Young makes no bones about the ravine's active complicity in the killings, writing of the murderer's "evil secret shared only by the ravine which had done nothing to give him away; which had, instead, covered his noiseless retreat with its own silent darkness, sucked all recognizable sign of his passing into its thick saffron slime, and, inanimate evil matching the animate, offered a dark, eager promise to do these things again." For Young, evil deeds require evil places. As a schoolgirl asks her art teacher moments before they come upon the body of her murdered friend at the bottom of the ravine, "You mean there are different kinds of darkness, Miss Warner?" "Yes," the young instructor replies, "there are different kinds of darkness."

AMY LAVENDER HARRIS is the author of *Imagining Toronto* which won the 2011 Heritage Toronto Award of Merit. She teaches in the Department of Geography at York University.

I

The ravine had been a point of dispute for more years than the town, which encircled it, could remember. For from time to time, appalling things occurred in its shaded depths, weaving dark strands of apprehension through the fabric of civic pride which had so far preserved it intact.

There were those who would like to have seen it stripped of every tree and shrub capable of casting a shadow. Those who had more than sufficient reason for loathing a tangled, cancerous growth, in places never pierced by the sun.

Another faction felt that partial denudation would be sufficient.

But the majority of the townspeople, whether motivated by love of nature or inertia, wanted it left exactly as it was.

At certain seasons of the year, as the sun sank towards the west, low ground mists gathered and thickened in it, to become part of a dusk which seemed never to have entirely withdrawn. Even in midsummer, night came early there, turning it into a gulf of dark purple shadows while golden light still struck across the town of which it was geographically the centre, and yet in a sense no part at all.

On foot, the ravine constituted for the active a short cut from one part of the town to another. One descended by car only if the floor of the ravine itself was one's objective. Since it was not, and never had been, a water course, heavy rains, finding no immediate drainage, tended to accumulate in sullen pools slow to disperse, and the flat portion of the road would become slimy with viscous yellow mud.

Perhaps it was this lack of fresh water which accounted for the absence of birds in the ravine. Whatever the reason, it was a phenomenon troubling to the imaginative who retreated instinctively from the further observation that it was a place avoided by wildlife of any kind.

Innumerable foot paths ran down its steep, heavily wooded sides to mesh at the bottom with a further network wandering aimlessly amongst trees whose trunks rose out of thick underbrush. But there was little evidence that anyone ever lingered there.

By day, a park-like contrast to the busy urban life surrounding it, it did not seem particularly large, but at nightfall it widened until the lights on either side were no more than small constellations pricking futilely at the fringes of an immeasurable darkness.

For most of the people of the town, even those who championed its continued existence, a descent into the pit itself would have seemed preferable to being in the ravine on foot after dark. Only the very young, the very strong, or the very reckless were ever foolhardy enough to risk such a venture.

Deborah Hurst had been both very young and very reckless on the April night when she had left the hospital grounds and gone down into the ravine to encounter violence in its most abominable form.

II

November of that year was a repetition of April. Brooding grey skies shortened days already short enough, and rainfalls of varying intensity kept pavements glistening wet, turning pedestrians into scurrying mushrooms beneath umbrellas they were unlikely to forget. Only the children, in their brilliant raincapes, seemed both physically and spiritually impervious to a seasonal depression which enfolded the town like a thick shroud.

At four o'clock on the second Tuesday of the month, the light of a sunless afternoon was already failing as Dr. Gregory Markham paused briefly by the window which overlooked the ravine from the end of the third floor corridor of the hospital. With a few minutes to spare before he was due in the operating theatre, he nevertheless felt no inclination to linger where he was. Since the night when Deborah Hurst's bruised and violated young body had been given to him to mend, the ravine had not been a prospect which pleased him in any way.

Tall and rangy in silhouette against the oblong of the window, he shortened the focus of his gaze until it rested on his own hands. Hands which had done all that had been required of them, all that needed to be done within his province. That this had not been enough, was no fault of his, he knew. Yet, as he turned abruptly towards the door on his left, a continuing mixture of anger and regret gave a bitter twist to his mouth which, though at all times firm, could also be gentle.

The alarm clock, set to remind her when it was four o'clock, took Julie by surprise.

Stepping back from an easel so placed that it caught wan light from both the north and west windows of the long room which was her combined studio and living quarters, she glanced at her watch for confirmation of something she could not quite believe. Two hours, she thought ruefully, and what have I accomplished?

Blue eyes narrowed between thick lashes, she subjected the canvas on which she had been working to a swift appraisal, and, hypercritical though she was, saw that she had actually accomplished a great deal. Rich with colour, a New England autumn glowed beneath the contrast of heavy clouds; a convincing landscape which cap-tured not only the beauty, but the nostalgia of the dying year.

Momentarily she regretted the self-imposed exile which robbed her of anyone with whom she could share the pleasure of achievement. Then, with a slight shrug, she stooped to put on shoes kicked aside earlier, and walked briskly towards the end of the room where bathroom and kitchen, side by side, completed the apartment. I must hurry, she thought, knowing that she must be at the school not later than a quarter past four, and that it would take her a full five minutes to get the paint off her hands, bring some decorum to her hair, and renew her lipstick.

Working on her hands with soap and pumice, she realised afresh how fortunate she had been to find a place so ideally suited to her purposes. She was close to the school at which she taught. The garage next door, only one storey

14

in height, did nothing to interfere with the north light she needed for painting, and gave her a convenient parking space at the back for a station-wagon which could not be left out overnight on Ravine Street. Able to get her breakfast and lunch at the counter of the drugstore downstairs, dinner was the only meal she needed to cook for herself. Refusing to dwell on her unreasonable dislike of the ravine which her west windows overlooked, she thought, I could not have planned things better if I had drawn a blueprint in advance. I have too much. I don't deserve it.

Holding a diploma from the Beaux Arts in Paris, and with no necessity to earn her own living, Julie often felt guilty about taking an obscure teaching job which some-one else might really need. Her only need, but nevertheless a compulsive one, had been to prove that she could pro-vide herself with food and shelter unaided. She could, she knew, have remained in New York and found a job with more status and more salary, but not one offering the same leisure and opportunity for the landscape painting which was the most important thing in her life. Even more important than staying with the extraordinarily young parents who might have protested against her going, and yet had not done so. To properly appreciate the unselfishness implicit in this lack of protest was to invoke the memory of tragedy which, though now five years old, still had the power to make her feel physically ill.

She had, in part, been escaping from this memory when she left home. That the avenue of escape she had chosen should lead her in precisely the wrong direction was something that neither she, nor anyone else, could conceivably have foreseen.

Tuesday, 4.00 p.m.
The *Courier* was an afternoon paper scheduled to reach the newsstands at four o'clock, and on that particular Tuesday nothing had occurred to interfere with the schedule.

There was, therefore, no reason for Tom Denning to linger in the deserted offices of the newspaper, but for the moment he could find no sufficient reason for going anywhere else. One long leg hooked over the arm of his chair, his red hair dimmed by a blue haze of cigarette smoke, he toyed morosely with the neat desk plate which labelled him managing editor.

From the early dusk in the courthouse square outside, he could hear the thin cries of the newsboys: 'Read all about it! Read all about it!'

'Read all about nothing!' he muttered savagely, and promised himself, as he did on an average of once a week, that he was going to get out of a one-horse town where the only news was that there wasn't any news. To compete with the morning paper on that basis was to die of creeping futility. Even the ravine had yielded little of any consequence for six months, and the *Courier*'s 'Abolish The Ravine' crusade which had increased circulation in the early summer was petering out, its once bright pennant tired and dusty.

When he thought of the ravine, Denning had an acute sense of frustration and failure. Ever since the rape case in April, he had been nagged by the knowledge that, with no encouragement from the police department, he had played a hunch and made a fool of himself. Sticking his neck out, he had authorized headlines containing more than a vague promise that the 'sex maniac' at large in the community would be caught. When it had become obvious that the police investigation was getting nowhere, an all-out effort had been made by the paper itself. A private detective had been hired, and a reward offered. At the end of a month the detective, having detected a little less than nothing, had been dismissed. The reward still stood, not because the *Courier* still cherished any hope of its being claimed, but because to have withdrawn it would have required print admission of its impotence.

'Read all about it!' 'Read all about it!'

If the kid had died, Denning thought dispassionately, he might eventually have been able to forget his ill-advised handling of the affair. But the kid had not died.

Tuesday, 4.00 p.m.

The lights in the entrance lobby of the hospital were already on when Mrs. Wylie, her movements as neat and economical as her neat, small, white-haired person, picked up her telephone and asked for an inside line.

'Mr. Jenks? Main desk speaking. Would you be good enough to switch on the outside lights now?'

'You know it's only just on four, m'am?'

Mrs. Wylie's voice, though light and musical, was authoritative. 'I know that, but I think it's time they were on. Thank you.'

Putting down the receiver, she looked across the black and white tiled lobby towards plate glass windows flanking revolving doors, and when the false twilight outside dissolved in a flood of white light a very real relief briefly disturbed the delicate mask with which she faced her world.

Now that she could no longer see the trees beyond the car park as a palisade of darkness, distinct in itself, she should have been able to turn her thoughts away from the ravine. But she found that she could not do this. The whole day had been, and still was, too similar to a day she would be unable to forget as long as she lived.

As if it were happening all over again, she saw her niece turn away from the desk with the beautiful grace of a thirteen-year-old who had been taking dancing lessons since she could first walk; saw her reach the doors and wave; saw dark curls, and a smile alive with mischief.

Her eyes bleak, she thought, I survived the loss of my husband in one war, the loss of my son in another. I twice found the courage to go on, God knows how. But

17

those things were merciful compared with this. Clare is grateful that her child survived at all. If Deborah had been my daughter, I would rather have seen her dead.

'An unpleasant day, Mrs. Wylie. Have there been any outside calls for me?'

Mrs. Wylie's hearing was excellent, but she often failed to anticipate this man's approach. He had, of course, come towards her from the private entrance, but this was no reason for not hearing him when she always heard everybody else.

'I don't think so, Doctor,' she said evenly. 'Just a minute while I check.'

Hatless, his dark hair sleek and shining beneath overhead lights, he waited with an urbane assurance born of a more than secure professional reputation. A slim man of medium height, his long, handsome face would not, in spite of his good looks, have been particularly memorable had it not been for the arresting singularity of eyebrows as white as his hair was black.

'No. No calls this afternoon, Doctor.'

'Thank you, Mrs. Wylie. I expect to be in the hospital until six o'clock.'

Turning to the call-board behind her, Mrs. Wylie pressed a button, and an illuminated arrow appeared beside the name of Dr. Norman Bartell.

Tuesday, 4.00 p.m.
The grandfather clock, an heirloom too large for the narrow hall in which it stood, had just struck the hour, four mellow notes, when Clare Hurst settled herself with her knitting beside the picture window in the living-room. A thin graceful woman, her brown curls dusted with silver, she was nearly fifteen years younger than the sister on whom she knew she at times depended too much.

The knitting was a pretence so patent even to herself, that she almost immediately let it fall, unheeded, to the floor. She was waiting for Deborah to come home, as she did every afternoon, seven days a week. She knew that, for her own sake, she ought not to do this. But she could not help it. With the first almost imperceptible fading of daylight, tension would begin to take hold of her, knotting the muscles at the back of her neck, sending tremors to the tips of fingers grown so painfully thin that her rings chattered one against the other. Then, all resolutions breaking down, she would go to the window, unfit to do anything else.

Briefly she considered calling her sister, simply to hear her voice. But private calls to hospital personnel on duty were not encouraged, and she knew the impulse was born of nothing more urgent than her own weakness. A weakness which occasionally, but only occasionally, made her regret having refused Beryl Wylie's offer to live with herself and Deborah after Tony died. Sisters, both widowed, it would have been the obvious thing to do, to join forces. But Clare had known that for herself and Beryl it would have been wrong, would have robbed each of them of an independence they cherished. Since an April night whose date was branded on her heart in pain which never entirely left her, she had realized even more clearly than before how right this decision had been. To have had anyone else in the house with Deborah and herself would have been to have undermined her courage rather than to have strengthened it.

How dark it is already, she thought. Thank God, Tony and I could not buy the house facing the ravine. I will concentrate on how glad I am that there are nice little houses across the street. I will think about the people in them, and what they might be doing now, and the time will pass—and she will come home. I will not think of Tony. Or if I do, I will try to think only that at least he has been spared what I have gone through, what I still face, day in—day out. I will think of Julie Warner, and what her friendship means to Deborah, and to me. Was I wrong to ask her to do the portrait? Perhaps I was. But I never had one, and now, in any ordinary way, it is too late.

So dark, so dark. I hate the winter which is coming, but even more I hate the thought of another spring. Dear God, if only I could keep Deborah here beside me, never let her out of my sight. But Dr. Markham is right. I can't keep her cooped up as if she were a baby. He said to let her go, that she would be all right. She has been. But how many years will it go on like this? How many years can I stand without cracking up altogether? In the beginning, Greg Markham seemed to think that there might be some hope... but now... now....

Shaken with compulsive sobs, she buried a ravaged but still pretty face in her almost transparent hands, drowning in darkness thicker than that of the approaching night.

Tuesday, 4.00 p.m.
The new public school stood almost in the shadow of the water tower, and, as the crow flies, directly across the ravine from the hospital. Its single storey U-shaped, it embraced a playground sheltered from the prevailing wind and designed to catch the morning sun. Desolate, rain-soaked, this playground now stood mute testimony to a sunless day, a long shaft of yellow light from the art room at the north-east corner emphasising, rather than reducing, its present dreariness.

Inside the school, echoes of the four o'clock bell still clung to fast-emptying corridors as Susan Philips and Barbara Grey dawdled their way towards the end of the north wing.

Susie and Barbara were 'best friends'. Living next door to one another in big houses, set in big gardens, on Ravine Road, they had shared small secrets ever since they could remember, and it was axiomatic that when Susie elected to join the late art classes Barbara should follow her lead.

At the advanced age of eleven, there was a pleasing sense of importance to be derived from membership in a class that was not a compulsory part of their education.

Hitching up a short plaid skirt which kept slipping down over hips which had yet to deserve the name, Susie said, 'She's beautiful, don't you think?'

'Who? Oh, Miss Warner. You bet.'

'Do you think my hair will ever get to look like hers? You know, sort of shining.'

Barbara gravely regarded her friend's mop of short, fair curls with some doubt, but said magnanimously, 'Well—it's the same colour.'

Giving her skirt up as hopeless, Susie's clear blue eyes gazed dreamily into a future in which she intended to wear tight black satin. 'Do you think Miss Warner has a Love life? I'm going to have a Love life.'

Barbara's reply to a rosy generality was characteristically practical. 'It's a good thing we're opposites, as well as being the same, if you know what I mean. What I mean is, you being a blonde and me being a brunette. That way we just naturally won't ever like the same boys. I mean, we'll never fight.'

'As long as I live, I'll never fight with you about anything, Barby. Cross my heart and hope to die.'

The acoustics of the school were peculiar, and Susie's last soft-spoken word was transmuted into a lingering whisper in the long corridor. But neither of the children, occupied with thoughts, to them of great profundity, noticed this.

They had reached the open door of the art room, when Susie, in an entirely different tone, said, 'Oh, I almost forgot! I've something I simply have to show you! Quickly, we've just got time if we hurry. It's in my locker.'

'What is it?'

'You'll see. Come on!'

Running down the stairs to the basement cloakroom

they wound their way in and out amongst a few last stragglers, but the cloakroom itself, when they reached it, was already empty.

Breathless, Susie opened her locker and fumbled in the pocket of a bright red raincape. 'It's an absolute secret. You're the only one who'll know. It's my birthday present for Mummy, and I bought it with my own money. I've saved for simply ages. Darn it, where—oh, here it is.'

Inkstained fingers treating a small packet with the utmost reverence, she unwrapped white tissue paper to disclose a very modest silver bracelet. 'There! Isn't it the most gorgeous thing you ever saw?'

'It's simply divine! Golly, won't she be thrilled.'

Carefully rewrapping the little parcel and putting it back in the pocket of the red raincape, Susie said, 'I just can't wait to see her face. I nearly didn't stay for art today, I was in such a hurry to get home. I'm not going to wait for after dinner, I'm going to give it to her the very minute I get in.' Pausing, she added slowly, 'I might even——'

'You might even what?'

Evasiveness was normally no part of Susie, but this was a sentence she thought it better not to finish, even to Barbara. 'Nothing,' she said airily, and was gone, slender legs flying under a whirl of plaid far removed in every way from tight black satin.

Tuesday, 4.00 p.m.

Some deep recessed mechanism, dissociated from memory which refused to function as such, always told Deborah when it was four o'clock, and therefore time to go home. Her watch which she still liked to wear, was of no practical value because she could no longer interpret what had become for her meaningless cabalistics.

In the past it had been the school from which she turned towards a bungalow no more than three short blocks away. Now, when her inner time clock sounded its warning, she might have wandered anything up to a mile from home. Whatever the distance, it was always made greater than it might have been by the devious routes she followed in order to avoid any sight of the ravine.

'Does she know she does this?' Clare had asked Greg piteously.

The surgeon had shaken his head. 'No. Not in the sense in which you and I understand the word.'

'Then how—why—'

Greg Markham had replied with the quiet conviction which had steadied Clare again and again when she had felt herself on the verge of toppling into the abyss which had claimed her young daughter. 'There is one thing, at least, of which I am quite certain. Deborah is completely insulated now from mental stress of any kind whatsoever. She never laughs, but remember, too, that she never cries.'

Deborah, Clare had thought, striving for control. My lovely Debbie whose laughter threaded itself through everything she said and did, even through tears that came and went like summer storms. Lovely, lovely Debbie, who had danced when she walked, who had feared nothing in heaven or hell, because she had never really believed in hell.

When Deborah, physically well, had first started to leave the house alone, she had been followed day after day; sometimes by Clare; sometimes by Greg, when he was free to do so. In this way they established the pattern of what she did, and was likely to do, reassured themselves that she was unlikely to come to further harm. In essence, she did nothing. She simply walked and walked, without destination or purpose, keeping away from the ravine, coming back for meals with curious robot-like precision.

To Clare, it was a pattern, no matter how painful, which seemed to contain no irregularities which could not be explained.

To Greg Markham, there was one small deviation which continued to bother him, which did not fit.

Deborah, when she walked, confined her aimless wanderings to the east and south sections of the town. Never once did she cross some private line of demarcation into the section on the west side of the ravine where the hospital was. Greg might have found this reasonable, within the twilight world of unreason, on the grounds that she had descended into the ravine from the hospital on the evening when she was so brutally attacked. The one contradiction to this theory was embodied, both literally and metaphorically, in the small person of Mrs. Wylie. Why, if Deborah had a subconscious horror of the hospital and therefore everything connected with that rainy April evening, was Mrs. Wylie, the last person to whom she had spoken, one of the very few people who could still evoke some kind of response from her? One could argue that Mrs. Wylie was her aunt, and so was accepted by Deborah automatically. A perfectly good argument, but Greg had not been able to satisfy himself with it. Under the circumstances it had not the necessary force. Yet if one did not accept it, one had to discard the whole hypothesis of the hospital itself being related, in what was left of Deborah's mind, to what had happened to her. Once one did this, the only possible explanation of her rigid avoidance of the area was that somewhere within its limits it housed the man she had cause to hate and fear above all else. If this were the case, it meant that she had not only seen, but recognized him.

'Read all about it! Read all about it!'

The further side of the courthouse square was the closest approach Deborah would make to the ravine, and this only because a statue of Lincoln and a formal planting of small trees seemed to increase her actual distance from it, made any accidental sight of it next to impossible, particularly when her head was turned away. Wherever she was, her head was always turned away from the ravine, even when it was blocks from her. This habit gave her an awkward, lopsided appearance which, coupled with her nervous, uneven gait, prepared passers-by in advance for her vacant eyes and slack mouth.

Most of the people in the town knew her, and her story. In the restaurants, the corner drugstores, the post office, the public library, even the churches, anywhere where people were accustomed to foregather with time on their hands, the sinister story of what had happened to Deborah Hurst had been discussed and rediscussed innumerable times. That it could happen again, these people knew perfectly well, yet as the months passed they thought less and less about this, until it became an eventuality they did not entertain at all. In accepting the vacuous stare of what they took for a hopeless idiot, they gradually forgot the pretty, intelligent face and mischievous brown eyes they had once known. Speaking to her as she passed, with offhand kindness, expecting no reply and getting none, they scarcely saw the silly half-smile which acknowledged a greeting without responding to it.

'Read all about it! Read all about it!'

Scuttling homeward through the early dusk of an afternoon which she did not know was a Tuesday, in a month which had no name for her, Deborah was no longer news; no longer of any compelling interest except to a handful of people who, for widely divergent reasons, rarely lived through any given day without thinking of her. Amongst this handful was one, totally unsuspected, whom any one of the others would give their lives to exterminate if offered the chance. But he had been as careful, that one, as he was perverted, his evil secret shared only by the ravine which had done nothing to give him away; which had, instead, covered his noiseless retreat with its own silent darkness, sucked all recognisable signs of his passing into its thick saffron slime, and, inanimate evil matching the animate, offered a dark, eager promise to do these things again.

III

The late art classes which Julie had undertaken on Tuesdays and Thursdays represented no hardship to her because she was passionately fond of children. Actually, in many ways, she found them the pleasantest times of the week. Removed from the more rigid context of the ordinary school curriculum, they allowed her to instruct and encourage the children according to her own lights, and to make friends with them in a way not possible when teaching thirty or more at a time.

Psychology, of an elementary kind, had dictated the separation of boys and girls into two groups. If she had not done this, and used for her Thursday class the lure of what might properly be considered 'manly' subjects, she suspected that she would have had very few volunteers from amongst boys of an age to consider art in any form as a sissy undertaking. Possibly because stuffed rabbits and old muskets had only a limited appeal for herself, she preferred Tuesdays and freedom of choice which allowed a spray of brilliant autumn leaves, or an opalescent piece of lustre ware; anything with colour. To Julie, colour was akin to music in that it stirred something deep within her, could fire her imagination as a thing-in-itself apart from the shape and texture of the object into which chance had woven it.

When, in early September, the principal of the school had first introduced her to the room which was to be her domain, she had been secretly amused by the great plate glass window set into the north wall. It had seemed to her an unnecessary affectation on the part of the architect, and a hideous expense for tax-payers unlikely to be rewarded by the miracle of another Botticelli, or even, to put the thing in a more proper perspective, another Rockwell Kent. Since then, however, she had been given reason to temper her amusement to some extent, for Susie Philips showed evidence of a quite exceptional talent.

The door at the end of the room, provided in order that sketching classes could be held out of doors without disturbing the rest of the school, Julie had approved of immediately, and it had stood open most of the time during the early weeks of the term.

Towards six o'clock on the second Tuesday in November, however, a cold draught seeped in under its lower edge, to trickle across the floor in small chill eddies, and the big north window was a pitch-black square which seemed to cast a shadow over the unrelieved white light within the room.

'Time to shut up shop, kids,' Julie said, and noted with some surprise that Susie had already begun to put her things away. Susie usually had to be pried from her paint-box by force.

Crossing the room, she stationed herself beside a long cork panel to which she tacked up paintings, not yet dry, as they were brought to her. Each effort received approbation, whether deserved or not. Julie believed in the stimulus of encouragement, and the results she obtained justified her belief. Added to her quick, warm smile, it was a policy which made her universally popular with the children.

Normally the class numbered ten, but with colds and flu thinning the ranks, today there were only seven masterpieces to pin up on the board.

The last one in place, Julie said, 'There! Don't they look nice? Now, collect your coats, and I'll be back in a minute.'

As she left the room, to find the janitor and tell him he could lock up, a hum of italicized conversation sprang up behind her. *Until I came here*, she thought, *I had forgotten how terribly important everything is when one is very young. The most trivial things, from an adult's point of view, give them such pleasure. This has been very good for me, has helped restore my perspective as nothing else could have done, has made it possible to remember Nina without always remembering how she died. Even knowing Clare and Deborah has not upset the balance these kids have restored to me just by being themselves.*

'Mr. Harmon! Oh—Mr. Harmon!'

Her voice echoed and re-echoed down the bright, empty corridor, eliciting no response, leaving, as the last echo died away, no sound other than the sharp click of her heels.

I might have known it, she thought. *He's probably in the far corner of the south wing, perverse old man that he is. Well, at least the kids should be ready to leave when I get back.*

'Mr. Harmon!'

That Julie should drive the children to their own doorsteps after the late classes had been her own idea, but one which parents as well as children had accepted with gratitude, particularly when the days began to close in early and six o'clock meant darkness often no less complete than that of midnight. For this reason, as much as any other, she had been glad of the decision which had led her to exchange an expensive convertible for the battered blue station-wagon which, while being much more suitable for a school-teacher, was also a great deal larger.

'Mr. Harmon!'

'That you, Miss Warner?'

You know damn well who it is, you old nuisance, Julie thought, wanting to laugh in spite of her annoyance.

Looking into the classroom from which his voice had come, she said, 'You must think walking is good for me.'

'Never hurts when you're young,' the old man replied, grinning.

'I'm not all that young,' Julie told him tartly.

'You through now, Miss Warner?'

'After ten minutes of playing hide-and-seek with you, I am, for your information, more than through. Good night, Mr. Harmon.'

'Good night, Miss Warner.'

Starting back towards the north wing, Julie heard him chuckling to himself, and though resignedly, next time he will probably be in the furnace room.

When she reached her own room again, she took her trench coat from its hook on the door, and was doing up the belt before she was struck by any discrepancy in the small cluster of children, ready and waiting. Quickly she counted heads. Six, where there should have been seven. No bright red raincape filled out a spectrum otherwise complete.

'Where is Susie?' she asked. 'Hasn't she come upstairs yet?'

From a group, if anything, too articulate, there was no response. And something not only in the fact of that silence, but in its quality, was acutely disturbing.

'Where is Susie?' she repeated, and her voice was sharper than she had intended.

The little knot of coloured rainwear seemed to tighten into closer formation, the shuffling of rubbers on the bare, board floor the only sound in a harshly lit vacuum unbroken by any other sound.

Singling out a figure in blue, and speaking more

gently, Julie said, 'Barbara. Will you please tell me where Susan is?'

'She—she's gone, Miss Warner.'

'But why?'

'Well, you see, she was in an awful hurry today. What I mean is, it's her mother's birthday.'

Don't be a fool, Julie cautioned herself. Because you are too vulnerable, don't jump to conclusions. 'What a silly child she is,' she said lightly. 'It's so much quicker by car. Come on, we'll catch up with her and take her home first if she's in such a special hurry.'

'Miss Warner——' Barbara's usually matter-of-fact young treble was hesitant, scaled down to a nervous whisper.

'Yes, Barby?'

'I think—that is I mean—I think she's taken the short cut.'

With an enormous effort Julie prevented her own sick alarm from communicating itself to the children. 'You think she was going to cross the ravine?'

'Yes.'

'Did she tell you so?'

Wide-spaced, honest grey eyes looked miserably into Julie's. 'Not exactly. But before, I mean before the class, she said something which—well, I just think she has.'

Julie knew Barbara, knew that she was not a child to indulge in baseless flights of fancy, as some of the other children might. Her mind racing, she thought, the road will be awful after so much rain, and that back left tyre, which I should have had changed, is too smooth, but I've got to do it, and I dare not leave these others. They would scatter like frightened lambs across the night. Fifteen minutes already gone. How fast can I get off without sending them into a panic?

'Come on,' she said gaily. 'We'll surprise that bad one! We'll take the short cut, too. But we'll have to move fast, or she will have got across before we catch up with her. Last one in the car is the cow's tail, and that counts me!'

Not only what she said, but the way she said it, was exactly right. The uneasy cluster broke up at once into chattering units scrambling to get through the door ahead of one another. And when, purposely the last, she slid in behind the steering wheel, a giggling chorus chanted, 'Miss Warner is the cow's tail—Miss Warner is the cow's tail!'

Although it was not actually raining, night air heavy with moisture made it necessary to use the windscreen wipers. And as she swung out of the school grounds on to the street bordering the ravine, a detached portion of Julie's mind noted that even Barbara, on the front seat beside her, would be unable to see road conditions which would have taken the edge off what she had for the moment managed to make into a game.

If we meet another car before we reach the turn-off, should I stop and ask for help? No. It would waste too much time. Julie—take hold of yourself. Nothing will have happened to her. Nothing will happen to her. You're not being rational. It would be too much of a coincidence if on this one occasion....

Yet, reassure herself as she might, in her mind's eye she saw a dark figure, faceless but with awful substance, lurking in the close-grown bottomland of the ravine, a shadow darker than the shifting, mist-filled darkness which concealed it. A small girl, her bright raincape robbed of colour by the night, would only have to go down into those depths once under such circumstances, and once would be too often.

They passed no other car, no living creature of any kind, on the short stretch of Ravine Street between the school and the road which plunged with steep abruptness into the ravine.

Changing into low gear, feeling the tyres spin as they

left firm asphalt to find an uncertain grip on wet clay, Julie said, 'Hold your hats, kids! Here we go!'

'Gee, it's black!'

'Nance, aren't you excited?'

'Can't we go any faster, Miss Warner?'

'Won't Susie be surprised!'

'Maybe she's got home already.'

'Maybe she's lost.'

'Miss Warner, how could she see where she was going?'

The car was too big for proper handling on cork-screw turns walled by tree trunks wetly shining as the headlights flickered across them. Needing every ounce of concentration for driving, Julie nevertheless knew that somehow she must answer, must continue to protect them from contamination by her own fears, born of such another night, which might in this instance prove baseless.

Her voice, light and easy, seemed to belong to a stranger far removed from the agony of the moment. 'She would be able to see the road. Not distinctly. But it would be a little less dark than anything else.'

'You mean there are different kinds of darkness, Miss Warner?'

'Yes,' Julie replied steadily. 'There are—different kinds of darkness.'

And this, she thought, is in all ways a kind I do not like. It has a dimension of its own in which it seems to have swallowed itself. It is a projection, not just of the night, but of this place which repels me as no other place has ever done before.

A branch scraped slowly along the side of the car to tighten nerves already taut, and she could feel the sharp edge of her teeth against her lower lip as she manoeuvred carefully around still another bend in a series which seemed endless. Yet the increasing reluctance with which the wheels pulled themselves free from the dragging clay told her that they must be approaching the end of the winding descent, would soon be on the short, flat stretch they would have to traverse before beginning a climb which would, she knew, be even more difficult.

Eyes straining to the outer edge of the swath of light ahead of her, she searched for the flash of red which would be the first sight of a little girl running home to her mother. Susie, if she had not started out by running, would be running now. Of that, Julie, in her knowledge of the child, was certain. Yet each twist in the sloping corridor down which they inched produced nothing but disappointment laced with mounting apprehension.

Side-slipping, the station-wagon slid down the final drop on to the level. If we don't find her here, Julie told herself, it will mean that she is probably all right. With the head start she had, she ought to be near the top on the other side by now. But something in the sodden silence of the ravine bottom strangled optimism, and in spite of the twittering talk of the six children so close to her, she felt that she had never been so alone, so entirely dependent on her own resources.

She was a good driver, who actually liked difficult driving, but when she saw the condition of the road ahead of her, she knew that she was probably beaten. Thick with slime, the ruts in places drowned completely in stagnant, muddy water, it was a tunnel offering a challenge so malignant she realized that luck, and little else, would get her through it.

'Miss Warner——'

This time she could not answer, could not divide her attention by even a fraction. Changing into second gear, accelerating as fast as she dared, she allowed nothing to exist for her beyond the small, brightly lit stage created by the headlights.

As if she were a built-in part of it, she felt the car

struggling for firm traction; was aware of the weakness of the left rear tyre, the tread almost gone; responded with the car as it picked up speed; felt her heart lurch, as the wheels lurched through standing rain water up to the axles; mingled the strength of her own fierce will with the straining motor as the front wheels regained comparatively solid ground.

The skid, when it came, was slow but deadly in its effect. Unable to counteract it, knowing that she must not use the brake whatever else she did, virtually helpless, Julie loosened her too tight grip on the wheel, and braced herself to do anything she could do if the big car threatened to leave the road altogether.

With gentle inexorability, the arc of brilliance from the headlights veered away from the narrow confines of the road. Moved across sombre trees whose leafless branches were lost in the night above. Approached the shaggy edges of a small clearing. Crossed this clearing. Picked up a thick growth of trees again. And came to a sharp halt as the car, having swung through a complete half-circle, caught and held in the deep-scored indentations of its own approach.

Julie, who should have been relieved, instead sat frozen to the wheel, her face drained of every vestige of colour. In a state of shock, she was briefly incapable of coherent thought or action. For, in the small clearing, she had seen what appeared to be the Devil himself, the black quintessence of all evil, with a spreading pond of blood at his feet. Reason screamed against the impossibility of such a thing. Yet, as though it were still before her, she saw, limned in sharpest detail against the dark backdrop of the night, the towering black figure, the contorted satanic countenance, and the brilliant pool of red.

'Miss Warner, have we had an accident?'

'We're turned right around the way we came from, aren't we?'

'I was scared a bit, weren't you, Barby?'

'I wish we could see out.'

'I guess we'll never catch up with Susie now.'

'Miss Warner, can we still catch up with Susie, do you think?'

Their high, excited voices, washing over and around her, brought Julie back to clear, cold sanity as nothing else could possibly have done. She had always been good in an emergency. She was superb in this one.

'No,' she said, without a tremor in her voice. 'I'm afraid we will have to let her get home without the surprise we'd planned for her. You see, we're having a bit of an adventure ourselves. We're stuck in the mud, and I'm not sure we'll be able to get out without some help.'

They were not stuck. And it had not been blood. It had been a red raincape. And she, Julie, was going to have to reach that red raincape and whatever lay under it as fast as she could, and alone.

'Look,' she said, 'I'm going to go and see if I can find a piece of wood to put under the wheels. That may do the trick.'

'I'll come with you,' Barbara said immediately.

'No. I have something else for you to do, and the others can help you. Do any of you know the S.O.S. signal?'

There was an eager chorus of assent. It appeared that they had all learned it at Guides.

'That's wonderful,' Julie told them, and meant it. 'Now I want Barby to sound it on the car horn, and the rest of you to count out loud so that she keeps it even.'

'There should be a little space in between each S.O.S. shouldn't there, Miss Warner?'

Julie, having found a flashlight in the glove compartment, laid her hand briefly on Barbara's shoulder. 'That's right, darling. Now, if it takes me a little time to find a piece of wood that's just right, you mustn't worry. Don't stop sending the signal, and whatever you do don't get out of the car. Will you promise me that you won't get out in this mud?'

Without reservation, they promised.

'Maybe we'll have somebody down here before you even get back, Miss Warner.'

Stepping out into the silent darkness, closing the door on a tiny world of life and movement, Julie prayed, O God, don't let any harm come to them. O God, let Susie be alive... don't let her be dead... not Susie...

Compared with the channel of light cast in the opposite direction by the headlights, her torch seemed dim to the point of uselessness. Common sense told her the dark shape which had been standing above the red raincape would be gone by now, would have melted into the surrounding night within seconds of her sight of it. Yet common sense was so small a part of the actual nightmare through which she moved, that she could feel no certainty of this.

Listening intently, hesitating when she had not intended to hesitate, she could hear nothing, either close to her or from further away. Smothered by foliage unhealthy in its density, few sounds ever penetrated this place from the town above. In her immediate vicinity the heavy silence was that of the grave. And as she stood there, the amorphous threat of the ravine itself pressed in against her, brushed the nape of her neck with a chill not born of the November night. A streamer of mist, slithering silently towards her, was the attenuated ghost of an old atrocity, long since forgotten by man, but still fondled by the ravine which had cradled its spawning. A ravine whose tangled, unhealthy growth bred atavistic fears in her stronger than her fear of a Devil who had at least been fashioned in the likeness of a human being, with arms and legs and eyes. Eyes, glaring out of deep-sunk sockets, which might even now be watching her. The thin wraith of mist was almost touching her. Without conscious volition she struck out at it. Sinuous, unbroken, it slid away from her.

Move while you still can, she admonished herself desperately. You have no choice. You must go to her.

Slowly she started away from the car, and was brought to a convulsive stop by the first blast of the powerful horn. Pausing to steady herself again, she listened to the repeated blasts, irregular in the beginning, and then settling down to a rhythm as automatic as that of a metronome. In one way, it was reassurance for her, was the hope that a patrol car would come down into the ravine before too long. In another way, it made what she had to do even harder than it had been, because there was no longer any possibility of hearing anything else.

She had not far to go. Moving now without hesitation, she was aware that one of her light shoes had been sucked from her foot by the clinging mud, but it was an awareness which failed to record the fact as of any importance.

Accompanied only by the steady blare of the horn, in itself an assault on nerves already over-taxed, she found the slippery verge of the road, skirted a clump of bushes which clawed at her legs in passing, and entered the clearing. A moment later she was on her knees beside a pool of red that, though not blood, might just as well have been. Glazed blue eyes stared up at her from a small face, lifeless and white, framed in fair curls sticky with clay. Clay which streaked a torn plaid skirt, and thin bare legs angled and graceless as those of a savagely twisted rag doll.

'Dear God——'

Fighting against dizziness which threatened to overwhelm her at any moment, Julie lifted a small hand, its fingers, even in death, still clenched in pain and terror, and felt for a pulse that did not beat.

There are other things I should do, she thought dully. I know she is dead, but there are things I should do, if only I could think of them. A mirror. But I have no mirror. The eyes. They say if you touch the eyes... can I do it?

37

She could. And she did. But how, she never afterwards knew.

To return to the car, to pretend, to protect the other children from knowledge which must not come to them just then, was, in an entirely different way, almost harder to do. But she did this, too.

She went back to them. She joked with them over the fact that she had not been able to find a piece of wood in the woods. She congratulated them on the way they had carried out her instructions. She allowed Barbara to go on with the signalling, knowing that if she were to have attempted it herself, she would have beaten the horn in a wild, patternless frenzy.

I cannot leave her lying there alone in the darkness, she though despairingly. She is dead. But I cannot leave her like that. Yet I cannot keep these others here much longer. Five minutes. If nobody has come in five minutes, I will have to get them out while I still have the strength.

Two minutes later she caught a glimpse of lights, intermittent flashes, seen and then not seen, as a car felt its way cautiously down the same torturous route which she had followed herself. With numb thankfulness she recognized the red blinker of a police cruiser.

'A rescue party!' she said, and, in spite of herself, her voice, until then under such perfect control, cracked a little. With a terrible effort, she steadied it, as she continued. 'We don't want them to get stuck too, do we? I'm going to go and meet them. You stay here, all of you, and we'll be out in no time.'

Walking along the road, she realized that she was only wearing one shoe, and, without thinking, stepped out of it and went on through ice-cold mud and water in her stockinged feet.

She met the cruiser a little more than a hundred feet from the station-wagon.

'Run into trouble, miss?'

'Yes.'

'What kind of trouble?'

'Murder,' Julie said, and though she was not cry-ing, tears were running down her cheeks.

IV

On Wednesday morning, the clouds, still unbroken, hung so low they seemed to rest on the triangle formed by the squat mass of the hospital, the gaunt height of the water tower, and the spire of the Episcopal Church facing the courthouse square. A sombre pall stretched from horizon to horizon, their funeral grey brooded over a ravine from which the scent of death crept up to spread into every cranny of the town.

Julie, who had not left the police station until midnight, and who had not slept until dawn, was wakened from uneasy sleep by the telephone and a request that she return again to the police station. Still fully clothed as she had been when she threw herself down on an unopened lounge-bed, she swayed on her feet with fatigue, thinking mechanically, I must bathe, I must change. It is nine o'clock, and there is no sun. No sun. No sun ever again for Susie. Dully she looked from her mud-stained bare feet to the mud-stained silk stockings lying in the middle of the floor. Caught in a trance between sleeping and waking, she thought, it has only begun. Until there is no sun for that devil, ever again, it will not be finished. Either he dies—or I do. There can be no other ending to this thing. Stumbling a little, her eyes refusing to focus properly, she crossed the room to her clothes-cupboard.

At the same moment, Tom Denning, on his way to the *Courier* offices, a morning paper stuffed in the pocket of his overcoat, came to a halt almost on the steps of the Episcopal Church while he concentrated on what a bloody fool he had been to have associated himself with an afternoon publication. And he, while his opponents scooped… he paraphrased wrathfully. Even the inquest, it seemed, tentatively set for Thursday afternoon, was not going to be fresh grist for his mill. Somehow, he promised himself grimly, the *Courier* was going to get a scoop out of this thing before it was over. Just how, he did not know. At whose expense, he did not care. A rehash of the Hurst case would be a start if he could dig up some striking similarities between the two attacks apart from the obvious ones of time and place. Before going around to the police station, a call to Greg Markham, though unlikely to be productive, might be worth trying. Instinct had always told him that Greg had held back in some way on the Hurst affair, but he'd be damned if he knew what there could have been to hold back.

Ramming a disreputable hat further down over his face, he moved on at a pace which covered the ground much faster than it appeared to do.

He greeted those members of his staff already at their desks with a growl, went through the outer office to his own glass-walled cubicle, and kicked the door shut.

His temper was not improved when he found that he could not get a line through to the hospital. Dialling again and again with irritable persistence, he unfairly pictured Mrs. Wylie engaged in a lengthy private conversation.

Beside Mrs. Wylie's neatly shod feet a crumpled newspaper lay out of sight, hidden by the built-in semicircular desk. Since taking over her post from the night supervisor she had had no respite. Although it was not yet the official hospital visiting hour, the red leather chairs on either side of the black and white tiled lobby were filled by people who knew that they would have to wait, and who had come in spite of this. The telephone had been ringing without pause, transmitting anxious inquiries most of which were totally unnecessary. It seemed that with the fresh tragedy in the ravine, the morale of the town had temporarily cracked, causing a general hysteria. Men and women, usually reasonable, were this morning belligerently unreasonable in their mass conviction that most of the patients recovering in the hospital must have suffered a relapse during the night. Doctors' bulletins, which usually satisfied them, now satisfied nobody. They insisted, where possible, on speaking to the doctor concerned in person, and then to the patient, in that order. It was as if death were a reality born only now of the night which had bred their needless personal fears.

Mrs. Wylie, who had hoped for a free minute in which to call Clare, a call which she felt to have some genuine importance under the circumstances, replaced the telephone only to lift it again.

'General Hospital, Main Desk. Dr. Markham? Who's speaking, please?' Her voice, automatically pleasant, had lost any trace of cordiality when she spoke again. 'He's very busy this morning, Mr. Denning. All right, if you insist, I'll see what I can do. Switchboard? Will you call the third floor and see if you can get through to Dr. Markham? Thank you.'

Greg, as he tossed a stained white operating coat across the back of a chair in the resident surgeon's office, knew that he was not going to like the job which lay ahead of him at the morgue. He could not, however, refuse the note he had found on his desk when he had come down from three consecutive hours in the operating room. 'Captain Velyan would appreciate it if Dr. Markham could go to the morgue at his earliest convenience. Homicide feels it would be of value to know if there are any marked similarities between the injuries sustained by Deborah

Hurst on April 17 of this year, and those which proved fatal to Susan Philips on the evening of November 22nd. If at all possible, Captain Velyan would like to see Dr. Markham in person at his office after the examination has been made.'

Greg Markham liked Velyan, and a sympathy existed between the two men based on mutual respect, and recognition in each other of sensitivity neither of them would have admitted to in words. This, combined with the courtesy of a message which could have been a direct command, had caused Greg to rearrange his schedule at some inconvenience to himself.

He was already shrugging into his overcoat when the telephone rang. If his had been any other profession, he would have walked out and left it ringing. As it was, he felt compelled to answer.

'Dr. Markham here.'

'Tom Denning, Greg. I hear Mrs. Philips has been brought into your place of business in a state of collapse. Can you give me a line on how she is?'

Frowning, Greg said, 'She isn't my patient, as you undoubtedly know.'

'I know, but you're probably in touch.'

'She isn't my patient,' Greg repeated tersely.

The staccato voice at the other end of the telephone remained unruffled. 'Close-mouthed bastard, aren't you?'

From the office window Greg could see a corner of the large white house where Susan Philips had lived out her too short span. He had never been inside that house, but in the early summer he had taken Susie's tonsils out. Anger flattening his syllables, he said, 'It's better than being another kind of bastard.'

'Hold it, chum, hold it. I'm only earning my living.'

Forcing himself to relax, Greg said, 'Sorry, Tom. Look, I'm pushed for time. Was that all you wanted?'

'Two more items. Brief. Do you feel there's any connection between this and the Hurst thing?'

'I have no facts in support of such a theory.'

'But you have some feeling about it?'

'I didn't say so.'

It was Denning's turn to show annoyance. 'If you're not careful, Greg, you're going to smother under the weight of that Hippocratic oath you insist on carrying around with you. All right, I know when I'm licked. Would it be ethical to tell me if you've ever met this Warner girl, and if so——'

But Greg, catching sight of a clock, had no more time to waste. 'We can discuss my ethics, and your lack of any, over a drink sometime, if you like. Right now, I have other things to do. Good-bye.'

Putting the telephone down, he did not realize that chance had prevented him from saying something he would later have regretted. Never having met Julie Warner, he would have said exactly that, and in doing so considerably narrowed her chance of survival.

On his way out, he stopped to speak to Mrs. Wylie. 'This will be very hard on Clare. How is she taking it?'

Mrs. Wylie spoke as quietly, and with as little emphasis as he had done. 'She called me at seven this morning, as soon as she had seen the paper. She is afraid to let Deborah out of the house.'

'Because she might hear about it?'

Mrs. Wylie nodded.

'There is no need to worry about that. Deborah walks in a world of her own. Nothing, not even this, will get through to her. You can give Clare all the assurance she requires on that score. At the moment it is Clare, herself, whom I am concerned about.' Taking a small pad out of an inner pocket he quickly wrote out a prescription. 'Get this filled, give it to her, and see that she takes some tonight. It will help her to sleep.'

The fine lines of Mrs. Wylie's delicately moulded face were no deeper than usual, but her eyes gave her away. 'I don't know why you should be so good to Deborah—to us, Doctor.'

His smile was fleeting, but it helped her through the rest of a day she would not like to have faced without some support from outside. A day in which memories she had been at pains to thrust away for six months crowded in upon her, their dark wings beating ruthlessly against an outward serenity she clung to more through force of habit than through any present strength. Deborah, as she once was, had been her hope for the future, as well as Clare's. Today she found it difficult to believe in any kind of hope for anyone.

Unsmiling now, Greg crossed the road to the car park on the edge of the ravine. He noticed that the space beside his car, reserved for Dr. Bartell, was still empty, but the chief object of his attention was the ravine. And as he backed away from the thick, unrevealing secrecy of evergreens choked in the grasp of maples from which the last sere leaves were falling, he cursed steadily under his breath.

Driving along Ravine Road towards the centre of the town through traffic heavier than was usual at that time of the morning, he managed to direct his thoughts away from his destination, but not so far that the connection between those thoughts and his present errand was not a close one. That a doctor, who allowed himself to become emotionally involved with his patients, would not last long, he knew, and normally his was an objective rather than a personalized sympathy. Deborah was a startling and continuing exception to this rule, the real reason for which he had kept even from Clare.

To have conceived any affection, in the ordinary sense of the word, for the awkward marionette with the imbecile's smile which Deborah now was, would have been quite impossible. But Greg, who had never laid eyes on her until she lay under the white light of the operating table, had nevertheless had one brief, never since forgotten, glimpse of the girl she had been.

He had been on late call on that April evening when the bruised and torn child had been brought into the hospital towards nine o'clock. It was eleven before, still under an anaesthetic, she was wheeled out of the operating room.

His job done, and well done, he should then have gone to bed. Instead, he went out to pace through the hospital grounds, smoking one cigarette after another in an abortive effort to dispel what was, for a moment, a taut, furious hatred of all adult humanity. Criminal assault was, to him, always horrifying, but when it involved a girl so young, a girl innocent and immature in all ways, it became the most evil crime in man's overstocked roster. Even the thought that he himself should belong to a genus capable of such bestiality temporarily revolted him. And, well disciplined though he was, he recognized in himself a desire for vengeance primitive in its force and violence.

Seeing nothing of the wet spring night, of the lighted gravel paths he followed, he might well have walked until dawn told him that that particular darkness of nature at least had passed.

What time it was when he saw the white glimmer of a nurse's uniform approaching him, he did not know.

'Doctor?'

Throwing away a cigarette, freshly lit, he replied at once, 'Yes? I'm needed?'

'No new case, Doctor. It's the girl. The special with her, Miss Smith, asked me to find you and tell you that she's getting restless. Miss Smith wasn't sure whether you wanted to see her again tonight, or not.'

'Tell Miss Smith that I will be there in three minutes.'

'Yes, Doctor.'

A single shaded lamp was burning beside Deborah's bed when he came quietly into her room. Crossing to her, he took her pulse, and laid his hand gently on a

46

flushed, damp forehead which jerked away from his touch as the dark head, eyes still closed in synthetic sleep, rolled sideways on the pillow.

Addressing the nurse who had been standing beside the bed, he said softly, 'Go ahead and get yourself a cup of cocoa. I'll let you know when I'm ready to leave her.'

Leaning on the rail at the bottom of the bed, immobile, alert, he watched as Deborah, stage by stage, struggled back to the surface of a fully conscious self dormant since some undetermined moment in the fight for life which, by some unexplained miracle, she had won. That she had been found in time, by two young toughs whom bravado alone had taken into the ravine, was another miracle in itself. To have lain all night in the freezing, rain-soaked gully where she had been discovered, would have been to complete the work begun by hands responsible, among other things, for the mottled bruises on her slender neck.

The decision to allow her to regain consciousness then was one which Greg took without prior intention. He did it because, with no conceit, he knew that he was better equipped than most, not only by training but by temperament, to deal with what would be, at best, a shockingly bad few minutes for this girl. Ideally, her mother should have been there, but Clare was temporarily too shattered to be of any real use. Still staggering from the shock of the car accident which had robbed her of her husband, this second blow had hit her too soon, too cruelly.

If his attention had wavered at all, he might have missed it. The fractional instant in which brown eyes, completely rational, their quick intelligence unimpaired, looked directly at him.

Afterwards, he at times had difficulty in believing that it had happened at all, so immediately had her retreat from the unbearable taken place. Without a movement of the eye muscles, without a flicker of an eyelid, all intelligence vanished from those brown eyes leaving nothing but the blank, uncomprehending stare of an amiable idiot.

Deborah Hurst, capable of remembering more than she could bear, had quite simply decided to remember nothing at all.

In the days that followed Greg told no one of this brief flash of lucidity, although his thoughts revolved around little else. Keeping the knowledge that her mind was not permanently impaired strictly to himself, he studied its implications from all angles. He saw at once that if she were to regain her memory, and if the man who attacked her were not a transient, he would make an immediate attempt to silence her for good. Stronger than she looked, she had fought like a young wild-cat; the kind of punishment she had taken, in part, gave ample evidence of this. Thus, it stood to reason that, in what Greg judged to have been semi-darkness, she had seen her assailant clearly enough to identify him if she ever returned to the world from which she had fled. As things were, her retreat was so complete she could pass him on the street without knowing him.

Greg's professional responsibility for her ended when she was no longer in need of surgical care. His moral responsibility, as he saw it, did not. Also, irrational as it seemed even to himself, that one instant during which he had seen her, as herself, had bound him to her, had left him with the unreasoning conviction that if she were ever to be cured it would, in some way, be through his instrumentation.

Before deciding definitely that surgery was his field, he had taken some psychiatric training, and when the psychiatric ward admitted failure in her case, he was not particularly surprised. In his opinion, prolonged treatment under the supervision of a really eminent man was her only true hope. That, or some entirely unforeseen set of circumstances so bizarre they would shock her back to reality in spite of herself.

He had been relieved when Clare accepted it as natural that he should take a part in watching Deborah when she first began to go out into the streets. To have shared his own special knowledge with her would have meant sharing it with her sister, and though he trusted both women's discretion, in their attitude alone they could not have helped betraying some belief in Deborah's eventual recovery. A belief of that kind, once it became generally known, might have constituted a genuine threat to her. As the weeks passed without incident, he was able to relax, to feel certain that she was perfectly safe in the cage she had built around herself. He even began to wonder if he had not lost his sense of proportion a little, and was being unnecessarily cruel in offering Clare no hope. Nevertheless, he continued to keep his own counsel, saying nothing to her either about the bank account which in time would be sufficient to pay for Deborah's possible rehabilitation, or about his reason for thinking that this might be successfully accomplished.

On the morning when he opened his newspaper to read of Susan Philips' death, and the manner of that death, he thanked his own particular gods that he had been so careful. For, even before he went into the morgue, there was little doubt in his mind as to what he would find there.

When he left the morgue towards noon, to walk across the square to the police station, he was no longer in any doubt at all.

Captain Velyan's office was a barracks of a room made pleasant only by the personality of the man himself. Greg, as he sat down on a hard, wooden chair opposite the desk, would have found it no more attractive than he had on any other occasion if it had not been for an elusive trace of perfume mingling with the ever-present cigarette smoke.

Smiling slightly, he said, 'You are accused of having closeted yourself recently with a mysterious lady visitor.'

Velyan's lined, dark face, lit by a pair of brilliant eyes,

lost a little of the brooding sorrow which was its most noticeable characteristic. A man whose compassion equalled his sense of right and wrong, he should never have exposed himself to the continuing disillusionments implicit in police work. Yet, if he had not done so, the cause of justice would have suffered instead.

His voice was deep and soft. 'Miss Warner. An extraordinary girl.'

'The school teacher?'

'A correct, but inappropriate label.' Then, without any suggestion of abruptness, he asked, 'You have been to the morgue?'

'Yes, and it was not nice.'

'No,' Velyan said quietly. 'Not nice at all. I'm sorry to have had to ask you to do such a thing. Did you reach any conclusions?'

'Yes. Very definite ones.'

'The same man?'

'In my opinion, yes.'

'Could you go into details on that, Doctor?'

'If you wish.'

Velyan sighed. 'I don't wish. Wish has nothing to do with it. Just a minute. I think we can spare you the necessity of appearing at the inquest if we get this down in writing.' Pressing a button under the edge of the desk, he looked towards the door, and when it opened, said, 'Would you ask Sergeant Bell to come in, please.'

A gruff voice, with a visible image of a salute in it, replied, 'Yes, Captain. At once.'

The willingness and promptitude of obedience which Velyan got from his men always impressed Greg. Velyan never ordered. He asked. But he got what he wanted when he wanted it.

Sergeant Bell appeared almost immediately.

'Doctor Markham, I believe you already know the sergeant. Sergeant, I want you to take down a statement which

I will witness, and which you will probably be called on to present at Thursday's inquest. Now you can go ahead, if you will, Doctor.'

Without hesitation or qualification, using the simplest language possible, the surgeon outlined the reasons for his own quite positive belief that Deborah Hurst and Susan Philips had, within the space of six months, been criminally assaulted and then strangled, in the latter case successfully, by the same man.

When he had finished, Velyan dismissed the sergeant, and then said, 'Is there anything you would like to add to that statement, Doctor, on a less official basis?'

Greg's grey eyes were ironic. 'If you ever have the misfortune to find yourself in *my* office, *you* will be seated facing the window.'

Pushing a crumpled package of Players across the desk, Velyan said, 'Help yourself. At least I'll have a view in that case, instead of a back alley.'

'Not a view to which I, at any rate, am partial now.'

'No. Perhaps my back alley is preferable, after all.'

'Infinitely preferable,' the surgeon said harshly. He took a cigarette, and lit it with deliberation. 'What I have to say now is not conjecture. It is fact. But fact which I think you will see some reason for not publicizing. The bruises on both these girls' necks have indicated a very accurate knowledge of pressure points. Too accurate to be coincidental. Once, possibly. Twice, no. You are dealing with a man who knows his anatomy thoroughly enough to be a most efficient strangler. I realize that this will not narrow the field appreciably, but it is, so far, the only specific evidence of any kind to come to light in either case. That is, as far as I know.'

'You know as far as I do,' Velyan replied sombrely. 'One obvious conclusion, for what it's worth, is that, since he didn't finish the job on the Hurst child, he must have been frightened off.'

'I reached that conclusion tentatively when I first examined her. Whether it was the boys who found her, or somebody else, who interrupted him, is something we can only guess at. But since the ravine is, to put it mildly, an unpopular place after dark, I think we can assume it was the two boys who saved her in every way.'

'And both of them have been in jail for petty thieving since then. It's an odd world.' Absently, Velyan stroked a deep crease running between his nose and his mouth. 'This similarity in the bruising is something that only you would have been in a position to recognize, isn't it?'

'Yes. The police surgeon had not reason to examine Deborah. He has only seen the Philips child. I have now seen them both.'

'You didn't mention the similarity to our doctor?'

'No,' Greg told him. 'I left that to your discretion.'

'We would work well together, Doctor,' Velyan said quietly. 'I think the possibility of a wandering tramp can now be wholly discarded.'

'Unfortunately, I'm afraid I agree with you.'

'So that if we don't crack this case, it is probably only a matter of time——'

There was no need for Greg to answer, and he made no attempt to do so.

'Well, Doctor, there's no reason for keeping you any longer. Thank you for coming in.'

Rising, Greg said, 'If you want me again, you know where to find me.'

And as he left the office, starkly functional in the grey morning light, he was again aware of the faint perfume he had noticed when he entered it.

V

Julie, returning to her apartment at noon after her second interview with a police captain whose quiet kindness was harder on her self-control than unfeeling brusqueness would have been, knew that to stay in the apartment through the twenty-four hours that stretched between her and an inquest she dreaded, would be the height of stupidity.

Working with feverish haste, she made a thermos of coffee, a few sandwiches, and collected her painting gear. It would be bleak in the hills, but anything seemed better than remaining in the studio to be haunted by ghosts, past and present.

On her way out of town, she passed the school, deserted, closed for the balance of the week.

In the hills, away from the town and the flat country surrounding it, she felt better. But when late afternoon drew in, she knew that she had done the preliminary work on a landscape as depressing as her own mood. Her camp stool folded and put back in the car, she stood for several minutes looking out over darkening forest slopes lit now by no more than a few last scattered touches of the vivid colours with which they had flamed so recently. Unable to refuse a symbolism she would have ignored if she could, she sought to escape from it by driving down a steep, curving incline at reckless speed.

Postponing the moment when she would be alone behind her own closed door again, she chose, contrary to her custom, to have dinner in the drugstore below her apartment. However, as soon as she sat down at the counter and gave her order, she realized that this had not been an entirely good idea.

'I guess you must still be feeling pretty bad, Miss Warner.'

'You guess correctly, Rosie,' Julie said briefly.

Rosie, who looked more like an English barmaid than an American soda fountain clerk, recognized no rebuff. Busy setting out knife, fork, and paper napkin, she went on, 'It's like as though there were a curse on this place. Me, I'm even scared on the street by myself now. A good thing we close here at eight o'clock, is all I can say. You wouldn't catch me staying out any later.'

'No mustard, please, Rosie.'

'Gee, that's right. You don't ever take it, do you? I'm real upset.'

Although she was the only one at the fountain, Julie was aware of other people coming and going behind her, and prayed that, if there were any whom she knew, they would leave her alone.

'There, that right, Miss Warner?'

'Fine, thanks.'

With nothing else to occupy her for the moment, Rosie folded plump white arms on the farther side of the counter, and leaned forward confidentially. 'Two of them reporter guys was around asking for you this afternoon, Miss Warner. One from the *Sentinel*, and one from the *Courier*. It was Mr. Denning himself come from the *Courier*.'

Startled, Julie stared at the girl. This was something which had not occurred to her. 'Oh, Lord,' she murmured.

'I told them you'd gone away some place, and probably wouldn't be back until tomorrow afternoon,' Rosie continued, looking pleased with herself.

'Thank you, Rosie. That was really good of you.'

'Well, I figured it wouldn't hurt you none not to see them. Nosey Parkers. Though, honestly, Miss Warner, are you going to go on staying in your place?'

'Why ever not?'

'Well, if it was me, I'd be real scared all alone the way you are.'

'I have nothing to be afraid of,' Julie told her crisply.

'Well, folks are different, I guess. Me, I'd be scared. You got to go to this here inquest tomorrow, don't you?'

Pushing aside a half-finished plate of food, Julie felt in the pocket of her trench-coat for her change purse. 'Yes. How much do I owe you, Rosie?'

'That'll be sixty-five.'

Julie put three quarters on the counter. 'Good night.'

'Night, Miss Warner. And thanks.'

Leaving the harsh white light of the drugstore, Julie turned right to skirt the building to her own door, and was sharply annoyed to find that mention of the inquest had made the palms of her hands damp with nervousness. Any infringement of her personal privacy bothered her disproportionately, and she dreaded the prospect of an ordeal which would require something other than physical courage.

Upstairs, she did not immediately switch on the lights, but instead walked slowly to the west window. Below her the sidewalk outside the drugstore lay as sharply defined as it had at noon. Across from her, the shadows of the ravine, contemptuous of a single street-lamp, welled up to flow in dark silence over the road. And as she stood there, a man, his identity made secret by the night, passed into the ineffectual orbit of the street-lamp and out of it again. And she thought, it could have been that one. It could be anybody. I saw him, but what I saw was not really a man at all.

With a quick jerk, she drew the curtains.

She had been in bed for more than an hour before she would acknowledge to herself that will power, unaided, was not enough to induce sleep, exhausted though she was.

I must sleep tonight, she told herself. I simply must. An awful montage of images, from which she could not shake herself free, going with her, she got up and went to the bathroom cabinet. Dropping a small yellow capsule into her hand from an almost full bottle, she hesitated, and then added another one.

Sleep came swiftly after that, but it was not peaceful. Tossing and turning restlessly, muttering broken phrases, she moved through the shifting layers of a dark dream in which two little girls, both fair-haired but very different from one another, fled ahead of her, always just out of reach of her own heart-breaking, desperate pursuit. Sometimes it was Susie, her plaid skirt whirling in her flight from death, who receded into a black tunnel from which she would never return. And sometimes it was Nina, blue eyes blank with terror, her shining Dutch cut wildly disordered, who was sucked into a night from which she did not come back. Nina, the little sister whom Julie, eleven years her senior, had loved as she might have loved her own child. Nina, who, on a cold winter night, had left the impressive foyer of a New York apartment house, a small violin tucked under her arm, and had never come home again.

Her long, slender body twisting against the pressure of blankets now wound tightly around it, Julie's whisper, even in sleep, was arid with too-well-remembered hurt. 'Nina... Nina....'

VI

Without committing himself to a definite decision, Greg had nevertheless known that, if he were free, he would go to the inquest. He considered it unlikely that he would learn anything of value that he did not already know, and yet it was too important a part of what had been made, in a sense, his business, to ignore completely.

That he should be three-quarters of an hour late was evidence of his mixture of reluctance and compulsion. And when he mounted the courthouse steps, he was intercepted by a police officer.

'I'm sorry, sir. No more room inside.'

'Does this make any difference?' Greg asked, and produced the police pass which he had found on his desk that morning. It represented Velyan's gently effective way of getting what he wanted without demanding anything, and Greg had greeted its appearance with wry amusement. He had not been asked to inconvenience himself by taking an active part in the proceedings, but he was unofficially invited to participate in spite of this.

Examining the pass, handing it back again, the policeman said, 'You'll have to stand, I'm afraid, sir.'

'That's all right. I don't expect to stay long.'

Officialdom lost a little of its self-conscious importance. 'They began to line up here at midday, sir. Had a bit of trouble when we had to start turning them away. Even brought their children, some of them, if you can tie that. I don't need to tell you that we didn't let no children go in.'

'People are inexplicable,' Greg remarked grimly. And, ignoring the resentful stares of a fair number who had chosen to linger around the door, he went through a dingy entrance hall, and from there into the crowded, and no less dingy courtroom.

Taking up what proved to be an excellent vantage point against the wall at the back of the room, Greg's first specific glance went to the coroner, for whom he had a little less than no respect at all. A stout, self-satisfied man in his early fifties, Dr. Pierce Wilmot devoted more time to political wire-pulling than he did to his practice, something for which, Greg thought cynically, the town could be grateful when it had a stomach-ache, but should regret at a time like this.

His attention shifting, he let his gaze roam over the sea of heads in front of him, assessing, amongst those he recognized, motives for their presence ranging from sensationalism and morbid curiosity to an interest painfully personal. Gordon Philips, a father who today might have been taken for a grandfather. The principal of the public school. Other members of the staff, and, he guessed, more of these whom he did not know. The parents of some of the children who had been in the ravine that night. Clare Hurst, her face haggard even in profile, seated beside the erect small figure of her older sister. All these had a very good reason for being there, for wanting to know all there was to know about tragedy which had already touched some, and represented a possible future menace to others. But when his survey reached the farther corner of the courtroom, and a sleek dark head close against the side exit, Greg's eyes narrowed in surprised speculation, for, in so far as he knew, there was no reason, morbid or personal, for the celebrated Dr. Norman Bartell to be wasting his gilt-edged time on something which seemed neither profitable nor any immediate concern of his. The corner where Dr. Bartell sat was in partial shadow, for no artificial light leavened the courtroom's dreariness, but Greg knew that he was not mistaken. He allowed himself to be distracted for a moment longer by a puzzle which seemed to be of comparatively minor importance, before turning his full attention to the blonde girl in the dark blue trench-coat who at present shared the spotlight with the coroner.

Dr. Wilmot coughed discreetly. 'Now you have given this court to understand that you drove these children home on a voluntary basis.'

'Yes.'

Dr. Wilmot's full-bodied, pontifical voice was inclined to boom slightly. Julie's soft huskiness, clear though it was, seemed by contrast to lack force.

'There must have been occasions when you did not do it, when you had—um—ah—private commitments which made it inconvenient.'

'No. There were not.'

'You mean that you never once failed to take any one of these children home?'

'That is correct.'

Dr. Wilmot cleared his throat with some authority. 'We can take it then that on the—ah—fatal night, there would have been no reason for any person to expect that Susan Philips would be alone on foot, either in the ravine or anywhere else. From this I think we can safely conclude that the—ah—criminal lunatic who perpetrated this outrage came upon this particular victim entirely by chance.' Pausing, as if in tribute to non-existent applause, he continued, 'Now, Miss Warner, painful as I know this will be for you, we will have to be a little more exact in our interrogation. On the Tuesday night under discussion, at what time did you first miss Susan?'

'A little after six o'clock.'

'Is it possible to be a trifle more precise, Miss Warner?'

Julie's hesitation was brief, but it allowed time for the growing tension in the court to be felt as a thing in itself.

'It would have been no earlier than ten past six, and no later than twenty past,' she said. 'But she—Susan—might have been gone anything up to seven or eight minutes before I missed her.'

'Would you mind explaining that?'

'It was my responsibility to find the janitor and tell him when the class was over.'

'Did this take any longer than usual?'

'Yes,' Julie replied, and thought, if old Mr. Harmon had not been so childish. If Susie had only told me she was in a hurry. So many 'ifs'... but I can't think of that now.

'When you did miss her, did you follow her immediately?'

'Yes.'

'But even so it must have taken a little time to collect the rest of your—ah—small flock?'

Pompous old wind-bag, Greg thought resignedly, and shooting a glance towards the press table set at right angles to the bench from which Dr. Wilmot presided, saw his opinion reflected on more than one face there. Tom Denning, he reflected, at the moment looked capable of murder, himself.

'It took perhaps another three or four minutes,' Julie said.

'And then how long do you think it took you to drive down into the ravine to the point where you made your—ah—very unfortunate discovery?'

Several years, Julie thought bleakly. But aloud, she said, 'The driving was very bad. Perhaps another ten to twelve minutes.'

Picking up a pencil, Mr. Wilmot made what he no doubt hoped the press would describe as 'a few lightning calculations,' before saying, 'Then we can assume, roughly speaking, that a maximum of twenty-five minutes, and a minimum of twenty minutes elapsed between the time when Susan Philips left the school and the time when she—ah—met her death. Which, taken in conjunction with the other evidence at our disposal, fixes the time of death at approximately six-thirty p.m.'

It was earlier when he got Deborah, Clare thought. Dear God, I should have stayed away from here. What made me think I would hear something, see something, that nobody else would notice? What could there be to hear or see? And even if there were something, what good could it do Deborah now? If every tree in the ravine were to be turned into a gallows, it would not help my Debbie.

Dr. Wilmot, perhaps ruffled that he had not made a greater impression with his somewhat obvious deductions, increased his volume of sound with his next question. 'What led you to choose the road into the ravine, Miss Warner, rather than what would have been your normal route?'

'One of the other little girls suggested that Susan had gone that way.'

'Did you understand from this other child that Susan had actually said so?'

'Not definitely.'

'Weren't you allowing your imagination rather free rein in acting so precipitously on a child's rather—ah—vague suggestion?'

'The facts would appear to prove that I was not,' Julie answered crisply, and with a great deal more assurance than she had hitherto shown.

A vague stir rippling across the courtroom was tangible proof of sympathy with her retort. And Greg, shifting his shoulders to a more comfortable position against the wall, thought, he deserved that, the bastard. But it wasn't wise of her. He'll make her pay for it, if he can.

His broad face flushed, the coroner reverting to a direct course of questioning, said, 'You reached the bottom of the ravine, Miss Warner, in time to surprise Susan Philips's murderer still on the scene. Is that correct?'

'That is correct.'

'You actually saw him in the beam from your headlights?'

'Yes.'

'Will you please describe in your own words what actually happened.'

Thrusting her hands deep into her coat pockets, hating all the eyes so intently fixed on her, Julie went back into the ravine. 'When I reached the level stretch of road at the bottom, I saw that the surface was very bad. I decided to go on, anyway. It was worse even than I had expected. I lost control of the car almost at once. It swung around in a complete half-circle, and it was as it swung that I saw—saw the man, in a small clearing at the side of the road.'

'If the car had not swung, you would not have seen him at all?'

'No.'

'You would have had no idea that there had been any—ah—tragedy?'

'No,' Julie replied, and for the first time volunteered to enlarge an answer. 'He must have counted on that,' she said slowly. 'That I should have seen him was accidental in every way.'

'How long did you see him for? A second? Half a second?'

'Less than half a second.'

'Then what did you do?'

'I got out—and went to Susie,' Julie replied woodenly.

'How did you know she was there?'

'I had seen, and recognized, her red raincape.' As if impelled by some force outside herself, to tell the whole truth and nothing but the truth, she added, 'I thought, at first, that it—was blood.'

Mrs. Wylie, scarcely aware of the sharp bite of Clare's fingers in her arm, thought, this girl has both more courage and more honesty than is healthy for her.

Dr. Wilmot's unctuous voice broke a silence oppressive in its intensity. 'A little fanciful, Miss Warner,' he remarked, and then realizing that he had again laid himself open to a return thrust, hurried on. 'You were quite sure, when you—ah—reached her, that she was dead?'

'Yes.'

'That is a difficult thing for a layman to be sure of, if I may say so, Miss Warner. How did you convince yourself of this?'

Julie's face had been white before. It was whiter as she told him what she had done.

An expert reluctantly giving ground, the coroner accepted what she said, and returned to the one really vital point in his witness's evidence.

'Now I would like you to describe, if you can, this man whom you say you saw.'

Captain Velyan, who, alone amongst those present, had some idea of what might be coming, sank lower in his seat, and fastened a brooding, unhappy gaze on the not too recently swept floor.

'I can't really describe him,' Julie said quietly. 'I can only give you my impression of him.'

'And what was that impression?'

'He looked like the Devil,' Julie replied.

'You mean he didn't look well?' the coroner asked smoothly.

A nervous titter broke out somewhere in the court, and was as quickly stifled.

Her chin held high, anger in the stiff set of her shoulders, Julie said distinctly, 'No, I don't mean that at all. I mean that he looked like Mephistopheles, like the Devil in person.'

Without even needing to look at a galvanized Press section, Greg knew that Julie Warner, if she had not been before, was now headline news. And though he was very sorry for her, he was also irritated that she should have fallen so far short of the favourable impression she had previously made on him. A comparison as far-fetched as this had no place in a courtroom, and the girl he had thought her to be would have known as much.

Julie's extraordinary statement had a very different effect on Mrs. Wylie. Although the delicate serenity of her expression remained unchanged, a quick pulse of excitement ran through her. To her it was the first clue to the shape and form of a man she hated as she had not known she could hate. Julie Warner had known what she was doing at all times during her ordeal in the ravine. Exhibiting remarkable courage and presence of mind, she had made no mistakes. On the basis of these facts, Mrs. Wylie saw it as perfectly logical to believe her quite literally. If she had seen a man who looked like Mephistopheles, then she had seen exactly that, and anyone who did not believe her was a fool.

That she was, in this case, surrounded by fools, was borne in on her as the interrogation proceeded.

'Making all due allowances for the—ah—artistic temperament,' Dr. Wilmot said, in a voice which indicated very clearly that he made no allowances himself, 'I must ask you, Miss Warner, to confine yourself to what you actually saw, not what you imagined you saw.'

Furiously angry, knowing that she had been made to look completely ridiculous, Julie nevertheless refused to back down. 'I have already told you what—I—actually—saw,' she said, her words deliberately measured and distinct.

Dr. Wilmot's shrug was decidedly theatrical, but general sympathy was with him now. The people, even the sanest of them, were thinking, a young artist letting

64

her imagination run away with her. Cool enough in an emergency, certainly, but not accustomed to seeing things as they really are. Too used to dressing an idea up in the bright colours of her palette, to be able to distinguish properly between fact and fancy.

Captain Velyan, still looking at the floor, thought unhappily, I warned her. It was all I could do.

Clare thought, it isn't fair! These people don't understand what she has been through. They don't know how good she has been to Deborah. They don't know about her sister. They have no right to judge her when she is trying to be honest, even if she is mistaken.

'Let us see if we can—ah—arrive at something a little more intelligible, if you please, Miss Warner.'

There were many replies Julie would like to have made to this, but she had the wisdom to make none of them.

'Can you tell us how this man was dressed?'

'Either in black, or some colour so dark it appeared to be black.'

'Thank you. That is more what we want. Was he wearing a hat?'

'No.'

'Can you tell us the colour of his hair.'

'Black. Obviously.'

Dr. Wilmot frowned. 'Why "obviously", if I may ask?'

Julie, no longer being wise, looked straight at a coroner whose thinning hair had never been dark. 'It is, I think, unusual to see a fair-haired devil.'

They had been too tense for too long, all those people packed into a confined space. Laughter, which they did not themselves find seemly, was a momentary relief to them.

Greg, although he did not actually laugh, smiled broadly, and thought, I wish I knew what to make of this girl. She neither looks nor behaves like a limelight seeker, and yet what else can explain the utterly preposterous stand she had taken.

'When you are ready, ladies and gentlemen.' The coroner vented his own irritation in a general reproof, and was rewarded by immediate silence.

Turning towards Julie, he said icily, 'I must advise you, Miss Warner, to restrain your somewhat ill-advised humour while you are on the witness stand.'

'I did not intend to be humorous,' Julie replied coldly.

There was no misinterpreting this reply, and the coroner's response to it was to attack her openly. 'You have given us so far some vague statements which can scarcely be regarded as a description of any value whatsoever. We have now, disregarding a so-called impression for which I am tempted to find a better name, a man in black, or possibly some other colour, with black hair. Or was his hair possibly some other colour, too?'

'No. His hair was black.'

Nobody will quite believe that, Greg thought sombrely, without realizing that he himself believed it. Our illustrious coroner has now succeeded in discrediting her completely. What price justice, when injured vanity can outweigh even the slimmest chance of identifying the animal who still walks amongst us.

'Did your "impression" include any idea as to his height?'

I can do myself no more harm than I have already done, Julie thought hopelessly, and for Susie... for Nina... I must tell the truth as I saw it.

'He seemed enormously tall. But I don't think he was.'

'Do you intend to contradict yourself, Miss Warner?'

'No.'

'Then what was your intention, if I may ask?'

'To tell you what I saw, and my interpretation of it.'

Secure in his personal victory, Dr. Wilmot pursed his lips, and allowed himself a smile which implied, what am I to do with this eccentric young woman? 'An "interpretation" is of even less value to this court than an "impression", I am afraid. Will you make an effort to be precise? Was he tall, of medium height, or short?'

'He was not short.'

'You can say no more than that?'

'No.'

The pontifical voice purred. 'In that case I see no need to take up any more of your valuable time, Miss Warner. Thank you.' Facing the courtroom, he continued, 'There will be a twenty-minute recess before proceeding with this inquiry.'

An immediate stir and shuffle followed this announcement, but Greg, unmoving, kept his eyes on Julie, while he thought with contemptuous disgust that Wilmot ought to be hung for throwing her to the reporters quite so flagrantly. Paying no attention to the people surg-ing down the aisle towards the main door and this unexpected opportunity to smoke and talk in the corridor, he watched as the press, Denning's red head in the vanguard, made a concerted rush towards the source of a sensation it intended to play to the hilt.

The scene as he saw it in the next quarter of a minute was to imprint itself on his memory, complete in every detail, for all time.

He saw Julie step down from the stand, and, desperate to escape, glance quickly around her for some exit other than the main door choked with people. Saw the *Courier's* photographer raising a flash bulb as he adjusted his camera. Saw a slim, dark-clad man, with sleek black hair, rise unobtrusively from his seat near the side door. Saw this man, beyond and well to Julie's left, turn briefly to look at her with a malignancy as unexpected as it was shocking. Saw the sudden white flare of a flash bulb, and a face—robbed of colourless eyebrows by blinding light that traced black shadows in the oblique furrows of a usually smooth forehead—which, for an infinitesimal fraction in time, might well have been the fact of the Devil himself.

67

VII

Frantic in her desire to get away, eyes seared by the cruel brilliance of the flash, Julie swung around just in time to see the side door open and close on the compact figure of a man in a dark coat.

Without an instant's hesitation, she turned and ran, and gaining the door undetained, did not know that for this she could thank a small, determined lady with white hair who had chosen to run interference for her.

A flock of pigeons, disturbed by the man who had left ahead of her, were circling above the statue in the middle of the square as, with flight her single clear aim, she turned, still running, down a side street. Only as she slowed to a brisk walk, did she realize that she had left the station-wagon parked in the square, and that she was headed away from her apartment. Bitterly, she recognized this as good fortune rather than bad, for the reporters, though balked at the moment, would undoubtedly make a beeline for her car, and after that for her home. Still angry, she wondered how long it would take to live down a truth so unbelievable that she had made a marked woman of herself in the telling of it. Captain Velyan had tried to warn her, and she had ignored his warning. Well, he had been right. She had known that her story might seem incredible. She had not dreamed that it could be made to appear so completely ridiculous. In part, she had a stupid, conceited fool of a coroner to thank for this. But she knew she had not improved matters by losing her temper.

Now what do I do, she wondered grimly. In advance, the inquest had seemed a definite first step in a definite direction. Instead it had proved to be a dead end. Raging inwardly, she thought, *why* couldn't they have listened intelligently? Why couldn't there have been at least one person who found what I had to say useful, who could have shown me how to use what I know? Where do I go from here in search of a devil that only I believe in?

Certain that she had, for the time being, eluded any pursuit, she did not at first pay much attention to the footsteps behind her. Then something in their positive authority alarmed her, and, without looking back, she cast around for a place in which she could seek temporary cover. This was a part of the town which she had never seen before, a dreary street, almost deserted at that hour, lined with drab shops and workingmen's houses. A combined café and bar, close ahead of her, held no attraction of any kind, but it offered a retreat from the footsteps rapidly overhauling her.

Opening a door plastered with worn cigarette ads, she found herself in a gloomy interior heavy with an odour compounded of stale beer and disinfectant. Again, almost running, she traversed its narrow length to a high-sided booth at the back, noticing as she did so that, apart from herself, the place was empty.

From where she sat, she could not see the door, but it was reflected with sufficient clarity in a cracked mirror above the bar for her to see the tall man in the grey suit who came through it, paused, then made his way directly towards her.

Everything I do today is wrong, she thought despairingly. I could have dealt with this much better on the street. Perhaps I can get out of here, even now.

But the man, sliding into the seat opposite her, and divining her intention, blocked it with cool effrontery so astonishing that she bit her lip to prevent an audible gasp. She could, she knew, have attempted to climb over the long leg braced against her side of the booth, but it would have been a proceeding so undignified she discarded the idea at once.

Her voice as icy as her blue eyes, she looked into the direct grey gaze of the stranger opposite her, and said, 'Would you please leave me, at once!'

'I'm sorry to force myself on you like this, Miss Warner, but I must talk to you.'

'I do not want to talk to you.'

'I'm afraid you have no choice,' Greg told her steadily. And looking up at the slatternly waitress who had appeared beside them, he said, 'Two coffees, please.'

'I don't——'

His smile transformed the gravity of his lean face '——want any coffee. Possibly not. But we must have some excuse for being here. Coffee, whether it's fit to drink or not, will provide that excuse.'

Suddenly terribly tired, Julie said, 'Please let me go. I have nothing to say to you, or to any reporter. Now, or later.'

'If I tell you that I am not a reporter, and that I have forced myself on you for your sake, and your sake alone, will you give me a few minutes in which to talk to you?'

'Why should I believe you?'

'Because I,' Greg replied with careful emphasis, 'believe you.'

'What do you mean?'

'I mean that I was at the inquest, and that I believe, without reservation, that the man who killed Susan Philips looked exactly as you described him.'

To Julie, it was as if she had been lost in a dark wood and suddenly felt the warm clasp of a friend's hand on hers. But, still raw from her experience on the witness stand, she searched his face intently before replying. His eyes encouraged her to trust him. And the set of his mouth seemed to promise that no confidence reposed in him would be misused.

'Who are you?' she asked finally.

'Gregory Markham.'

Startled, Julie had no time to enlarge on this. 'Then you are the surgeon who looked after Deborah!'

'How did you know that?'

'Because I know Clare—and Deborah.'

Watching her, he asked, 'Is it possible for anyone to know Deborah now?'

Although she already trusted him more completely than she quite realized, Julie did not want to discuss the macabre commission she had undertaken for Clare. That was Clare's secret, and shared only by Deborah who had spoken no single word to anyone since she had been carried up out of the ravine and a night whose dark fringes still imprisoned her.

'It was good of you,' she said quietly, 'to go to so much trouble just to tell me that you believed me.'

'You don't feel that many people did?'

Julie's smile was wry. 'Do you?'

'No. Which is fortunate, although you may not see it that way.'

'I don't see it that way.'

'You wouldn't,' Greg said. From a distance he had thought her unusually attractive, and had admired her courage. At close quarters, even though he had yet to touch her, she stirred his senses as few women ever had. What happens to this girl is going to matter to me, he thought. It already does. How can I best protect her, when she will do nothing to protect herself?

The waitress came back, put two thick white mugs of coffee in front of them, and went away again.

Julie pulled a menu card towards her, turned it over, and idly began to draw with a pencil her fingers had encountered in her pocket. 'I'm glad you believe me. But I didn't accomplish much, did I?'

'You may have accomplished more than you think.'

'How?'

Wishing he had had more time in which to prepare his approach, he thought rapidly, she is safe for the moment. Safe as long as she does not recall one single detail beyond those she is already aware of remembering. A one in a million chance has put me in possession of knowledge which, because nobody would suspect I possess it, is not dangerous to me until I find some way of acting on it. For her, it would be highly dangerous.

'You haven't answered my question,' Julie said. 'And your coffee is getting cold.'

'It is drinkable?'

'No.'

'Then I suggest we have a cigarette. Sometime I would like to take you to a place where the coffee is drinkable. If I may?'

Without looking up, Julie said lightly, 'You may. Sometime.'

'When?'

She did look up then. 'Aren't you moving a little fast?'

'I don't think so. Do you?'

Her pencil wavering briefly, Julie tried to refuse both his eyes and his question, and failed. 'I don't know.'

'Will you have dinner with me tonight?'

'I don't know. Please, Dr. Markham, you haven't told me how I may have done some good today.'

This much I will have to tell her, Greg decided. 'By having said what you did say in my hearing.'

The planes of her face seemed to become finer drawn, and the quality of her attention changed its character completely. 'You are telling me that it means something, something definite, to you?'

'Yes.'

Her voice expressionless, Julie asked, 'What?'

'I'm afraid I can't tell you that.'

'You mean you won't.'

'I can't burden you with something it is much better for you not to know. I followed you not only to tell you that I believed you, but to beg you to add nothing to the statement you have already made.'

Frowning, Julie said, 'But I have nothing to add. If I had anything else to say, I would have said it.'

'I know you would,' he told her sombrely. 'You would have put a gun to your head and pulled the trigger if you thought it would help. Well, that is more or less exactly what I do not want you to do. Something more may occur to you, and I want your promise that if it does, you will come to me before going to anyone else. The police, or anyone.'

Shielding her eyes with her lashes, Julie pretended to concentrate on a drawing which was purely automatic, which she did not really see herself. He is trying to protect me, she thought, this man who disturbs me more than I want to admit. And anything he tried to do will be difficult to block. God knows, I don't want to be hurt. Who would? But I must act as I see fit, and I can take care of myself. Can I pretend to go along with him, and get away with it? I am not good at pretending, and no good at lying. Somehow, I don't know how myself, I must hold the key that could close a prison door. If this man knows as much, then there must be at least one other who, if he does not know it, fears it—or can be made to fear it.

And thinking this, Julie felt the dark shadow of the ravine, temporarily held at bay, creeping across the town towards her, slithering beneath the closed door of a side street café, to curl its invisible menace around her, a cloak within whose folds she shivered involuntarily.

Greg, who had made a shrewd guess at the line her thoughts were taking, saw the shiver, quickly repressed.

'Julie——'

To have protested, even for form's sake, against the familiar use of her name, would have been stupid, would have been to deny something between them undeniable. 'Yes?'

'You will give me your promise?'

Not to tell anyone anything else before I tell it to him? This might not commit me too much. But I can not commit myself at all. 'No,' she said. 'I'm sorry. I can't make any promises to anyone. Not of that kind.'

'Look,' he said urgently, 'will you try and see this thing in some sort of proper proportion. Hunting murderers is not your vocation, and you are not equipped for it. That is a job for the law, and in this town the law, under Velyan, is intelligent and capable.'

'It is not the first time this had happened. It is the second. How capable does that make the law?'

'They are still more capable than you are,' he told her steadily. 'All crimes aren't solved, and this is a particularly difficult kind of crime to bring home because it is not generally committed by a criminal who can be recognized as such. A criminal of this type is a pathological case whose behaviour in all other respects is probably quite rational. There is no set pattern to his outbreaks. He takes nothing away with him by which he can be traced. He strikes in places where there are unlikely to be any witnesses. A dark alley. A deserted piece of woodland.'

'Or a ravine,' Julie said without emotion.

'Or a ravine. It happens at some time or other in almost every community. There is no reason why you should make this your personal crusade, and every reason why you should not.'

'I'm sorry,' Julie said. 'I cannot agree with you.'

That further argument would be a waste of time was only too obvious. But it was a defeat he was not prepared to accept passively. 'Are you really sorry not to agree with me?'

74

'Yes.'

'Then will you prove it by having dinner with me?'

'You're not being very fair, are you?'

'Not very,' he told her calmly.

'If I say yes, will you stop trying to look after me?'

'I'll make it less obvious, at least.'

Not to have to eat alone in the apartment, or to face the curious stares in the drugstore—Julie knew that there was nothing she would rather do than have dinner with him. But all she said was, 'All right, if you like.'

'I do like. Will seven-thirty be all right?'

'I'll be ready then,' Julie said, and, with flick of distaste, brushed a fly away from the menu card in front of her.

Caught by the sudden movement of her hand, Greg's eyes dropped to a drawing which, once looked at, left him taut with shock.

'Give me that thing!' he said sharply, and before she had time to know what he intended, he had taken it from her.

Black on white, precise, beautifully detailed, she had sketched the face of a man who was evil incarnate. The cheeks sucked in by a contraction which forced cheek-bones into undue prominence, the hooded glaring eyes, the oblique black eyebrows running up to the black hair-line—these things were the repellent, stylized character-istics of Satan as he is most often envisaged. But the straight nose with the flaring nostrils, and his sensual mouth with its well-cut but curiously flat lips, were the recognisable features of an individual man.

'Great God! Julie, did you know you were doing this?'

'I don't know. I suppose so,' Julie said indifferently. 'I'm always drawing something. It isn't very pretty, I grant.'

'Not very pretty!' With enormous difficulty he kept his voice down. 'It could be your death warrant!'

'Greg—really! It's just an impression of an impression I gave to some two hundred people not more than an hour ago.'

Leaning around the side of the booth to make sure that the place was still empty, the man, though assured of this, nevertheless turned the sketch so that it could not possibly be seen by anyone who might unexpectedly approach them.

'Julie. Listen to me!'

The grimness of his tone communicated his urgency to her, although as yet she had not fathomed its cause. The drawing was repulsive, she knew, but then the original, which still hung before her as though a hidden machine had stopped time itself, had been repulsive beyond any true description, spoken or visual.

She could draw this face just once again, Greg thought, and once might be enough to cost her her life. A remarkable artist with a photographic memory, she would, given a pencil, probably have difficulty in disguising what she saw even if she wished to. Tormented by vistas of a world in which pencils were scattered everywhere, waiting for a slender hand to pick one of them up, to begin absently on a duplication of the wicked, revealing portrait in front of him, he silently cursed the laws and conventions of a century which would not allow him to lock her up against her will.

'This is not just an impression,' he said evenly. 'It is, in part, a portrait of a particular person. But because of the angle of the light in which you saw him, and the inhuman expression on his face at that moment, it does not look like him at all. Only an unusually observant person would be able to see through the devil to the man. It is possible, even probable, that you might pass him on the street, yourself, without knowing him again. But if the man himself were ever to know that you had seen him clearly enough to make a sketch like this—I don't think you would live long after that.'

I should be afraid, Julie thought dispassionately. Perhaps I am. But not for myself. 'I'll be careful.'

'And you won't leave a paper chase like this behind you?'

The strength of his awful disgust showed in his eyes, as he looked again at a devil whose identity shocked him beyond any measure so far known to him.

Julie's negative was very definite. 'I will not.'

Taking out his wallet, Greg folded the sketch, and put it away with care.

'Are you going to keep my "death warrant"?'

'For a few hours only. Then it will be burned.'

He isn't quite certain, after all, Julie thought. He is going to check what he suspects. But it will do me no good to ask him how.

Greg, although absolutely certain, was going to check. He looked at his watch, and said, 'I must go now. First, however, I'll take you home.'

Leaving a place they would neither of them be tempted to revisit, she told him, 'You don't need to take me home. And, anyway, you have no car here.'

His evident surprise as he realized that this was so, amused Julie. 'Prominent young surgeon abandons patients, black bag, and new Buick in pursuit of glamorous witness.'

Greg fell into step beside her. Smiling, he said, 'It isn't a new Buick.'

'What is it, then?'

'An old Buick,' he told her, his smile broadening.

By the time they reached the courthouse square, the thing which really occupied their thoughts was further forced upon them by external factors.

'Read all about it! Read all about it!'

Instinctively Julie drew closer to the tall man beside her, seeking protection from the occasional covert stares directed at her from the stream of people through whom they were now moving. This is only a foretaste, she thought. By tomorrow they will all be staring. There will be nothing new in the *Courier* this afternoon. It must have gone to press too soon for that. But the *Sentinel* in the morning will have devils with bells on. Oh, God—why did this particular thing have to happen to me? Anything else—but not this.

'Read all about it! Read all about it!'

A thin drizzle had begun to fall, hastening the dusk, as Greg drew Julie's arm silently through his, and led her towards the maze of cars parked around the statue of Lincoln in the centre of the square.

'You have not coat,' Julie said quietly.

'It's in my car. Here we are now.'

'Please. My own car is here. I would rather take it.'

With obvious reluctance he let her have her own way. 'You're going straight home?'

With a flash of impatience she immediately regretted, Julie said, 'And if I weren't?'

'I know. It would be none of my business.'

'No. It wouldn't. Not yet——' Then she was gone, leaving him uncertain if he had heard and interpreted her last words correctly, but certain that to follow her and ask her would be to invite their complete denial.

There was still daylight of a kind when he swung into the hospital car park. But night had already fallen in the ravine, and white markings on black asphalt were blurred by its encroaching shadow.

Crossing the lobby from the private entrance, he was disappointed to see that Mrs. Wylie was not at the desk. That she was never there on Thursdays, he knew quite well. Today he had forgotten this.

'Any calls for me, Miss Benson?'

'Yes, Doctor. Out Patients has sent what they think is an emergency appendix up to Operating for further examination. The patient in 303 would like to see you. And—just a minute, I think there was something else. Yes, there was a call from Mrs. Hurst. She wondered if you could drop in sometime this week. She said it was not at all urgent.'

78

'Thank you,' Greg said. He knew well enough why Clare would have called, and it had been his own intention to see her as soon as he found the time.

He realized, as he turned away towards the elevators, why he missed Clare's sister Mrs. Wylie. In a sense he did not know her well, knew nothing of her personal likes and dislikes, had no idea what she did with her time when not presiding over the main desk. In another sense he knew her better than he knew some of his most intimate friends. Linked to her in sympathy ever since the night when he had first seen Deborah, he had come to know what kind of person she was, to appreciate the unyielding calibre of a strength which might otherwise have remained disguised from him by her small, polished elegance. She was someone who could be counted on in any kind of emergency. And, absurd though this seemed, her presence at her usual post would have given him a feeling that the thin cordon of protection around Julie Warner was stronger than it had been.

It was half-past six before he was free to go to his office. Closing the door behind him, he locked it, something he could never remember doing before. Testing the lock, satisfied that it was efficient, he took Julie's 'portrait of a devil' from his wallet and placed it on the desk under a strong reading lamp. After this he shifted his attention to the bookcase and a collection of medical journals through which he leafed for some time before discovering what he wanted. Then, with the concentration he might have given to slides under a microscope, he studied both the sketch and a photograph in a publication more than a year old.

A casual glance would have seen no resemblance between the two. A more minute scrutiny, disclosing an almost exact duplication of nose and mouth, could still lead to the conclusion that this was coincidence. An unlikely one, but nonetheless a coincidence. In the case of the long, suave face of the photograph, one was continually distracted by the curious white eyebrows, both striking and unexpected in an otherwise saturnine countenance; eyebrows, moreover, which emphasized the unlined height of the forehead above them. To look at the sketch was to be struck by black, satanic eyebrows, and held not by the features as such, but by the appalling malignancy of their expression.

Very slowly, Greg closed the journal and replaced it in the bookcase. To have looked as closely into the face of the man himself, as long as his guard was up, would have been to achieve as little. The evidence was there, but only someone who, like himself, had seen that expression and the deep, distorting furrows which Julie had taken for eyebrows, would accept it.

Deliberately he tore the drawing into tiny pieces, placed it in a large copper ash-tray, set fire to it, and watched until it was no more than a smouldering heap of ashes.

Then, switching off the light, he crossed to the window, and, his hands gripping the sill with a force that made the tendons stand out, stared down at a lighted parking space bounded by the rampart of the ravine's close-grown verge. Deborah, after leaving her aunt, must have crossed that bright oasis of light, plainly visible—a lamb to the slaughter. Deliberately reckless, excited by her own daring, she had probably felt no more than a nervous quickening of the blood as she descended into virtual darkness, and an area forbidden to her, when alone, at all times. With Susie it had been different. Susie had felt she had a reason for doing what she did, but there could be little doubt that she had been frightened, really frightened, from the beginning.

Two already. And in time, unless he could find some way of preventing it, there would probably be another. The seasons would chance. The townspeople, all but those few who had been closely touched by it, would gradually forget the horror. In the ravine, the trees would thicken undisturbed. Parents and children, preoccupied with small, mundane matters, would grow careless. Then it would happen again.

To Greg, it was like looking at the preview of a film whose unprintable script he alone could revise. With cold objectivity, he recognized a responsibility which, if it went for long unrelieved, might quite easily break him. It was up to him to do something. That much he saw. At the moment he could see no further than that.

His study of the two pictures, if it had done nothing else, had at least given him some real assurance that Julie ran no immediate risk. As long as she kept quiet, and resumed her life in the ordinary way, he felt now that she was reasonably safe. The man, who in his perverted conceit had attended the inquest on his own victim, would never have seen himself as she had described him, would probably be revelling even now in the irony of a description which, from a purely factual point of view, might lead anywhere but to himself.

Thinking of this man, and his hideous appetites, Greg wondered why a crime, in all ways so repulsive, should seem even worse because it had been committed by a murderer who was well dressed, well washed—possibly even perfumed. A derelict, as bestial in his uncleanliness as in his unnatural lust, would have been somehow less shocking. He knew that, as a doctor himself, he should be able to objectify a psychopathic deviation from the normal, should be able to look on it with much the same scientific detachment with which he looked at a diseased leg. This was quite impossible. Hatred, he could, to some extent, avoid. Anger and disgust were unavoidable, were, if you liked to look at it that way, a sickness deep within himself which would only be cured by the obliteration of the cause.

His attention to the scene below him sharpened suddenly, and his hands tightened on the window-sill until the knuckles cracked.

Foreshortened by height and distance, a compact figure, moving with characteristic cat-like tread, traversed the car park to be lost on the outer edge of light which betrayed the cars in that spot by no more than a dull gleam of chrome and glass.

Not until some minutes after he had seen headlights come on, and a car back out and circle on to the road, did Greg turn away from the window. As he had not before, he now saw how easy it must have been to escape from the ravine on both occasions. As easy as it had been to descend into it.

VIII

When Clare reached home after the inquest, she immediately lit a fire in the living-room, and drew chairs close to it for herself and her sister. But though the fire burned brightly, it did nothing to dispel a chill which was not physical.

That the house should have been empty on her return, had not surprised her. It would have been more surprising to have found Deborah home at that hour. Nevertheless, she had looked through all the rooms before sitting down with Mrs. Wylie.

Holding her thin hands out towards a blaze which did not warm them, she said, 'Greg Markham didn't come back after the recess.'

Mrs. Wylie's glance was thoughtful, penetrating. 'I didn't know he was there at all.'

'He was standing at the back. He came in late. Beryl—am I an awful fool if I call him?'

'Not if it would help you in any way.'

'But you can't see that it would be of any real help, can you?'

Mrs. Wylie shook her head. 'No. He has already done all he can do. You can't expect him to perform a miracle.'

Her movements too quick, too nervous, Clare reached for the box of cigarettes on the low table between them.

'I know. I know. And yet somehow I go on expecting that he will do just that—perform a miracle.'

'Clare, dear.'

'You believe I'm crazy, don't you, Beryl? Well, perhaps I am. But I have a feeling that if anyone can ever do anything for Deborah, it will be Greg Markham. No one else.'

Compassion in her eyes, Mrs. Wylie said nothing. There was nothing to say that had not already been said a thousand times. Her own respect for the young surgeon's ability equalled her sister's, but she did not believe that he, or anyone else, would ever be able to restore Deborah to the sane and normal world. In her work, she often saw examples of blind, impossible faith in doctors. Clare, she felt, was too intelligent for this.

Clare's unexpected smile mocked herself as much as her sister. 'You don't need to tell me. You think, and have thought for some time, that I suffer from a virulent case of doctor-worship. Well, you're wrong. It's even worse than that. I think I have second sight. And my second sight tells me every day of my life that, with Greg's help, I will get Deborah back again—my Deborah—not the poor, voiceless, mindless creature who now masquerades under her name. That's why I continue to bother Greg, why I trade on a kindness which should have washed its hands of me and my child long ago. That's why it's a contact which must be kept alive. That's why I'm going to call him now—now when he cannot help but be thinking of Deborah.'

Alone by the fire, when Clare had gone to the telephone, Mrs. Wylie allowed herself to sag a little, and then, with a determined effort, pulled herself erect again. If only there were something I could do to help, she thought impotently. Something positive.

And she, who never swore, murmured fiercely, 'I feel so damned useless!'

Clare's light touch on her shoulder startled her. 'Talking to yourself, darling?' Clare said. 'You mustn't start doing that. You mustn't start getting queer, too. Because you're not useless. Far from it. At times you are my only strength, the support without which I might have gone to pieces over and over again.'

Recognizing the truth of this, knowing that, so much the older of the two, she had always been able to help Clare when she was in trouble, Mrs. Wylie nevertheless found small comfort in a role essentially passive. 'It isn't enough,' she said with unusual vehemence. 'I need to do something definite for you and Debbie.'

Her expression remote, unfathomable in the firelight, Clare said slowly, 'Perhaps you will be able to. Because you, also, are a part of my second sight.'

IX

Tom Denning, slouched in his car outside the drug-store above which Julie lived, was on the point of giving up what appeared to be a fruitless vigil, when he saw the blue station-wagon pass by and turn in on the far side of the garage next door.

Uncurling his long legs in a flash, he was out of the car and already leaning lazily against her door when she appeared at the further end of the alley.

Julie, seeing him, halted abruptly, her heart beating uncomfortably fast. Then, recognizing him even in the poor light as one of the press men from whom she had fled earlier in the afternoon, she drew a deep breath, and walked firmly up to him.

'Excuse me, but that is my door you're blocking,' she said coolly.

'Awkward of me,' Denning replied, with a grin.

'Awkward for you, if you don't move.'

'I hear the thunderous approach of conscientious cops. Exit one unwanted newspaperman, with more than his dignity bruised. Look, Miss Warner, you're news any-way. Wouldn't it be reasonable on your part to take some hand in the way you're presented to your public?'

'I don't imagine, Mr. ——?'

'Denning. *Courier*. Managing Editor. At your service.'

'I don't imagine, Mr. Denning, that you allow the people you interview to write their own script.'

'I might. In your case.'

'And then again you might now. I'm not a fool, Mr. Denning.'

'No. I don't think you are. But what you did this afternoon, if I may say so, was somewhat foolish.'

If I let him irritate me, Julie thought, as he is quite obviously trying to do, I will probably say something I will regret. Which is just what he wants. Keeping her voice level, she said, 'Then why not tell your readers just that. Tell them I was foolish, and see how interested they are in that news item.'

Damn, Tom Denning thought. She's right. She isn't a fool, after all. Then why that crazy rigmarole about devils? Maybe there's more here than I counted on. Maybe....

He changed tactics completely, and said in quite a different tone, 'I'm sorry, Miss Warner. I'm afraid I've let myself get into bad habits. One tends to, in my kind of job. I apologize for that last remark.'

Julie, who had expected to be addressed as 'sister' at any moment, was almost caught off base. Almost, but not quite.

'I accept your apology, Mr. Denning. And now, if you don't mind, would you let me past. I'm very tired.'

Well, for God's sake, he ejaculated to himself. The biter bit! She's called my bluff. Denning, if your long nose isn't doing you dirt, there's more news value in this girl than anyone suspects. If the *Courier* were to back her up, to start a state-wide search for a man who really does look like the Devil? I wonder. Play it smart, Denning, and let her go until you've had time to think this one over.

'Certainly,' he said, stepping aside as he said it. 'It was a crummy thing to do. To waylay you like this after what you went through in court this afternoon.'

A trifle disarmed, Julie said, 'Never mind about it.'

'It's just that this ravine business has hit me where it hurts.'

Julie was fitting her key into the lock. 'Oh?'

'Perhaps you don't know about the *Courier*'s "Abolish The Ravine" campaign?'

'No, I don't. I haven't been here very long.'

Wishing he could see her face better in the thickening twilight, he did his best to sound both straightforward and deeply moved. 'It hasn't been a very successful campaign so far. Couldn't get the people sufficiently worked up about clearing out the bloody place. Then a dreadful thing like this happens again. First Deborah Hurst—and now this nice kid.'

Julie had her door open, but she hesitated on the threshold. 'If I thought that I could help——'

Done it, Denning thought exultantly, but he took care not to let his jubilation show in his voice. 'I think you've helped enough already, Miss Warner.'

'Well——'

'If anything occurs to me, I'll let you know.'

A picture horrible in its vivid reality appeared in Julie's mind. A picture of something which had not even happened yet—but which could happen. 'Please,' she said urgently, 'if you do think of any further way in which I could help——'

Don't let yourself be coaxed, Denning. You're a man of principle. Don't start betting on two pairs, when you can still call for more cards. 'I'll let you know, Miss Warner. Sorry again for having barged in on your life on quite such flat feet. Good-bye.'

'Good-bye.'

The lower door could be locked only from the outside, an eccentricity which had never before particularly bothered Julie. Even now, she could not see that it mattered very much, for the door at the top of the stairs was a stout one and equipped with a new Yale lock.

As she went slowly up the stairs, she thought, there must be some way in which I can make immediate use of what I saw. Some way in which I can save another Susie, another Nina. Greg saw something in that face I drew which meant more to him than it did to me. It can't be anything other than a recognizable feature, or features. Not enough, perhaps, to add up to conclusive evidence. But enough, if handled properly, to bring a murderer out into the open.

Although she did not yet know what she could do with the little knowledge that Greg seemed to regard as such a dangerous thing, she did know what her only starting point must be.

Throwing her coat over a chair, pulling curtains and turning on lights with quick impatience, she turned to her easel and lifted down the half-finished canvas it held. A drawing-board placed where the canvas had been, she tacked a sheet of fresh white paper to it, and picked up a black charcoal pencil. Forty minutes before she need think of dressing for dinner with Greg. Time to spare for what she wanted to do.

Concentrating on a satanic mask, more than life size, which began to grow though the medium of charcoal bold and harsh in its certainty of outline, she duplicated the drawing which Greg, in another part of town, was at the same moment destroying.

And as she worked she listened for a sound which, if it were to come at all, would come soon. Her nerves, rasped by the implications of what she was doing, became tight with every street noise and every vibration from the drugstore below. But the stairwell outside her door remained silent, brought no echo of the faint, persistent scratching which she never liked, but today actually dreaded. I'm a coward, she though, but right now it would be just too much, the one thing I really could not stand.

Why Deborah should scratch at the door panels,

rather than knocking, nobody knew, least of all, probably, Deborah herself.

In the beginning Clare had brought her daughter to the studio. That after a time Deborah should turn up of her own volition, unaccompanied, was one of those unexpected quirks for which neither Clare nor Julie could find any explanation. Because Julie's door was the only door anywhere, other than her own, up to which Deborah would sidle and scratch for admittance. To Julie, the unique trust which this implied, was not sufficient recompense to offset the eerie silence, broken only by the sound of her own voice, which filled the studio when Deborah and she were alone there together. Yet, understanding only too well what Clare must be suffering, she had not the heart to protest against this unforeseen change in an arrangement at best deeply disturbing. To have let herself in for it in the first place, she knew, had been foolish, but with her background inevitable.

Grimly putting the finishing strokes to flat lips almost feminine in their sensual clarity of curve, she thought, I am caught in this thing because of the kind of person I am, as much as by the evil chance which has involved me. I don't want to do what I am doing for Clare, and she made a refusal easy. But I did not refuse. I don't want to oppose Greg. And yet I cannot help myself.

Thoughtfully, she studied the devil she had again re-created, and knew that neither hand nor memory had faltered. What her next step would be in a plan as yet unformulated, she could not tell. Dinner would provide the break she needed. Later she could think. And a warm tide of something more than gratitude flooded through her as she thought of a man whom she felt she knew far better than their one meeting warranted.

She was ready and waiting for him when he came exactly at the time he had suggested. Greg, when she opened the door to his knock, stood stock-still while he took in a picture of her which he did not want to forget. Blue eyes. Blue dress. Golden hair. And barbaric gold jewellery.

Very deliberately, his smiling eyes challenging her to refuse the tribute, he whistled.

Julie laughed, in spite of an effort not to. 'Behaviour unbecoming to a gentleman.'

Greg moved forward into the room. 'If you were under any misapprehension that I was, or would behave, like a gentleman, you must lay the blame entirely on your own over-hasty conclusions. I never made any such claim.'

'No?' Julie replied, still laughing. 'Not even after draping yourself in a cloak of mutual acquaintances, not to mention a four-storey hospital? Very thick sheep's clothing.'

His voice teasing, he said, 'You wouldn't want me to go on carrying a load like that around at the end of a hard day, would you?'

'If that's what constitutes a hard day for you, doctor, then your day isn't over,' Julie retorted crisply.

'And I thought you were a kind girl.'

'Your mistake. I'm a nice girl.'

'Not the same thing?'

'Not the same thing at all.'

To kiss her now, Greg thought, would really be a mistake. With an effort, he shifted his attention to the brilliant canvases lining the walls. 'These are all your work, aren't they?'

Julie, knowing perfectly well what he had been thinking, followed his lead with some relief. 'Yes. Part of the exhibition I hope to have next spring.'

'They're damn good, as I suppose you know.'

'I'm glad you think so,' Julie said. And she really was glad.

Looking around him, Greg saw a long, low-ceilinged room, with soft green curtains masking two large expanses of window, one of which he knew must face the ravine. Comfortable, modern furniture made it pleasantly livable, but on the whole it was, with the vital exception of her paintings, impersonal.

'This is not home to you, is it, Julie?'

'No. Home as you mean it is in New York.'

He guessed, correctly, that the security of both affection and money lay behind her, and wondered if there were any way at all of persuading her to return to that security. His judgement told him that she was probably safe enough where she was, but he had learned that to rely implicitly on judgement was to ignore the vagaries of a human element which, in this particular case, might prove quite unpredictable.

'I'm ready to go, whenever you——' Julie began, and broke off as she heard a gentle knock.

She walked across to the door, saying over her shoulder, 'It's probably Rosie, the girl who works at the soda fountain downstairs. She sometimes comes up for a few minutes when she has her time off. I'll tell her I'm going out.'

Her sharp gasp of surprise brought Greg to her side in two long strides. He found himself looking down at a small girl with grave, unsmiling dark eyes, and neat, dark pigtails lying against a schoolgirl's plain navy coat.

'Why, Barby,' Julie said softly. 'What a nice idea. Come in, darling.'

Exchanging a lightning glance of understanding with Greg, Julie drew Barbara into the room.

'I didn't mean to interrupt anything, Miss Warner. I mean, I don't need to stay at all.'

'But of course you'll stay a little while, after having come so far. Do you know Dr. Markham?'

'Yes. How do you do, Dr. Markham.' Politely, Barbara held out her hand.

Greg took the small hand in his. 'I have quite a wide

acquaintanceship amongst the younger ladies of the community, haven't I, Barbara? The only odd thing about this being that none of them seem to have any tonsils after having met me.'

The solemn, dark eyes reflected a ghost of a smile. 'We don't blame you, Dr. Markham. I mean, I know we're really better off without them.'

'Sit down, Barby,' Julie said. And continued apparently casually, 'Did you come to see me about anything special, or was it simply a nice idea?'

Sitting on the very edge of the chair she had chosen, Barbara said vaguely, 'I just wasn't doing anything. I mean anything important.'

'Does your Mummy know you're here?'

'Well, not exactly.'

'How exactly, darling?' Julie probed gently.

'Well, I was at the library. I mean, she knows I'm out.'

The library, Julie knew, was a long way from her apartment. She was wondering what she should do, when Barbara's voice, thin with desperation, drove all other thoughts from her mind.

'She'll never have them now, Miss Warner! Never.'

Aware that Greg had moved quietly to the other end of the room, Julie asked, 'Who will never have what, Barby?'

'Susie. She'll never have a black satin dress and a Love life. And she wanted them so much, Miss Warner.'

In one flowing movement, Julie was on her knees beside the child, her arm around shoulders rigid beneath the navy-blue coat. She has come to me, Julie thought, instead of her mother, because I was there. We are bound together, this bewildered little girl and I, in a way that can never be fully clarified to anyone else. We both loved Susie. We were both there. It is very simple, and not simple at all.

'Look, Barby,' she said slowly, 'what you say is true.

She won't have those things. But you must look at it another way. There isn't a doubt in the world that she has been spared a lot of unhappiness, too. Anyone with as much imagination as Susie had, who felt things as much as she did, would have been very miserable sometimes. You're rather miserable just now, aren't you?'

Silently Barbara nodded.

'Well, Susie's lucky in one way, darling. She won't ever have to know what it's like to lose her best friend. She won't ever suffer again, in any way at all. And when you think of her not having her black satin dress, remember at the same time that it might not have made her happy, that it probably wouldn't have made her happy. Black satin dresses don't usually make people happy.'

The grave eyes never left Julie's face. 'I never thought about it like that, Miss Warner. She won't ever have to worry about passing exams, either, will she?'

'No. She won't ever have to worry about anything any more.'

'Do you think that she, Susie I mean, would have got to heaven yet?'

'I'm sure of it,' Julie said clearly.

'Then I guess it's just me I have to be sorry for. And I shouldn't do that. I mean you shouldn't be sorry for yourself.'

'No, you shouldn't. But no matter how brave you are—and you are brave, Barby—sometimes you just can't help it. Look, I have an idea. Do you think I might be sort of an honorary best friend just while you get a bit used to not having Susie around? On Saturdays and Sundays I go up into the hills to paint, and I'm often quite lonely up there all by myself. Would you like to come with me, whenever you have nothing in particular to do?'

'You're super, Miss Warner,' Barby said simply.

If this baby of ten—or is she eleven?—can control herself so well, then I can too, Julie told herself fiercely.

Forcing a very natural smile, she said, 'Then that's settled. I have the most enormous beach umbrella you ever saw, quite big enough to keep the rain off two people, if it should happen to rain. And a picnic basket with two sets of everything in it. And lots of extra paints and brushes if you felt like doing some painting yourself. Later on we'll talk about the kind of sandwiches you like best. Right now Dr. Markham and I are going to whisk you home before anybody discovers that you aren't at the library.'

They put her between them on the front seat of a Buick which Julie noticed had no appearance of being old. And as they followed the winding road around the ravine to Barbara's house, Greg drew on the fund of stories with which he was accustomed to amuse and distract young patients in the hospital.

Julie, keeping her face averted from the ravine on her right, thought, I'm doing what Deborah does. They should fit us both with blinkers. But when she looked down at Barbara, and found her smiling, her own face cleared.

When they reached Barbara's home, Greg got out, and said very formally, 'May I escort you to your door, Miss Grey? Someone told me once that a gentleman always escorts a lady to her door. And I'm trying very hard this evening to convince Miss Warner that I'm a gentleman.'

Barbara giggled. 'You're making fun of Miss Warner, not me, aren't you? Good-bye, Miss Warner, and thanks for everything. I mean it won't be so bad now. I mean you've made it different, somehow.'

Watching them go up the walk to the house, their figures dark in silhouette against a brightly lit portico, Julie felt a tenderness, embracing both the tall man and the small girl, so piercing it made any other emotion she had ever known trivial by comparison.

When Greg got back to the car, he made no comment, but his hand found hers and held it. They stayed like that,

95

without speaking, for several minutes. Then his mouth was against hers in a kiss brief but possessive.

More shaken than she had guessed she would be, Julie drew away from him, and said uncertainly, 'But it can't happen like this?'

'It has happened like this.'

'Greg——'

'Yes?'

'You'll have to give me time to get used to it.'

'All the time in the world,' he told her gently. 'Which is not as chivalrous as it sounds, because I don't believe it will take you long.'

He took her to a restaurant in the foreign section of the town between the railway station and the corner of the courthouse square where the Episcopal Church, staunch bulwark of an older New England, blocked any further encroachment in that direction. He could well have chosen Minelli's for its food alone, and the distinctly European leisure which allowed patrons to eat at nine o'clock, or later, without finding this eccentric. Tonight it offered the further advantage of being as far removed as was possible, metaphorically at least, from both the ravine and the community as Julie knew it. She might be recognized, but she would not be stared at.

Looking at her, seated across from him at a small table covered with a green and white checked cloth, seeing her relax visibly, he knew that he had been more than right in his choice. And when she picked up the menu from its place against a straw-covered Chianti bottle, there was no pencil in her hand.

'Greg!' she exclaimed. 'They have canellone.'

'It's very good here, too. You like it?'

'Like it! I have a passion for it. There's a place in Florence, I don't even remember the name, but it's on the river not far from——'

'The Berchielli,' Greg cut in, smiling.

'Oh, no! You haven't been there, too?'

'Often. That is, as often as a pre-med student in Geneva, without much time or money, could get to Florence.'

'What did you go there for?' Julie asked, smiling. 'The food or the paintings?'

He returned her smile. 'At the risk of spoiling any good impression I may have managed to make on you, I must be honest, and say—both.'

During dinner they discussed paintings, medieval and modern, her delight in his knowledge of her own major interest very evident. And from there, wandered through talk about music and books.

Seeing the shadow of too well remembered horror recede and finally disappear entirely from her vivid face, Greg allowed himself to relax too. Deeply satisfied that her likes and dislikes should so closely match his own, he thought, she must have known other men, but it would never have been anything tawdry. She is alive and passionate, but her mind would always control her emotions. With her, it would never be emotion for emotion's sake. I have waited a long time for this girl. Now that I have found her, I am going to look after her whether she permits this or not.

Julie's slim fingers played with the stem of her wine glass. 'There must be something we don't agree on, Greg?'

Greg, who was facing the door, swore softly under his breath instead of answering. He should have remembered that it was Tom Denning who had originally introduced him to this place.

'Look,' he said quickly. 'A man I know has just come in. Don't contradict anything I say, or infer. Please.'

He had time for no more. Scarcely time for that much before Tom Denning, who could not possibly have missed seeing them in so small a place, ambled over to their table.

'Good evening,' he said, his eyes roving speculatively from one to the other of them. 'Any objection to my joining you a few minutes?'

Greg's face was unreadable, but the line of his jaw was pronounced. 'At the risk of a beautiful friendship,' he said lazily, 'I do object. Three, in this particular instance, would be a crowd.'

Not at all abashed, Denning said, 'Old friends, I take it? Objection sustained.'

'Julie and I don't get much time together,' Greg told him casually.

The speculation was still there, but it had undergone a change. 'Okay, pal. I have no taste for gooseberries, myself. See you around, Miss Warner.'

Damn it to hell, Greg thought violently, as Denning moved away. For one glance at Julie's face was enough to tell him that the damage done to their earlier mood could not be repaired.

Julie looked at her watch. 'It's getting late, Greg,' she said quietly. 'I should go home.'

He did not try to dissuade her.

As she went out on to the street, Julie felt miserably guilty. I should, she thought, tell Greg that I met Tom Denning this afternoon, but I know I'm not going to. And I'm not going to because there is, after all, something on which we do not agree. Very soon we are going to agree on it even less than we do now.

When they were in the car, she said, 'Do you like that man?'

'Yes and no,' Greg told her. 'He can be amusing, and he is highly intelligent. He is, on the other hand, entirely unscrupulous by any standards which I am prepared to acknowledge.'

I can believe that, Julie thought. But anyone who wants to get rid of that abominable ravine is on my side of the fence, whether he has scruples or not.

They arrived at her apartment too quickly, although neither of them said this aloud.

'One door is enough for any gentleman,' Julie said.

'You don't need to come up the stairs.'

'And lose the chance of proving myself twice over? I'll come with you. And there will be no attempt, gentlemanly or otherwise, to see your etchings.'

As they went up the stairs, Julie said, 'Why did you give Mr. Denning the idea that we had known each other for a long time?'

'If he were to know that we had never met until today, he would neither eat nor sleep until he found out not only how, but why, we met. He is the ears, eyes, and nose of this town personified. Once he knew how we had met, it wouldn't take him long to guess that I believe in your devil. It's common knowledge that I have a continuing interest in Deborah Hurst. If it were to become known that I was, through you, also taking an interest in the death of Susie Philips, it would be worse than unfortunate. That is the crux of the thing, Julie— the fact that it is through you.'

Because he would not be there in another minute or two, the apartment looked bleak and empty to Julie. 'And you still won't tell me what it is that you guess, or know?'

'No.'

'Do you think that's fair, Greg?'

'It may not be fair, but it's safe.'

'Do you think I give a damn about my own safety?'

'No. But I do.'

Without going on with it, Julie knew that nothing she could say or do would shift him from this position. Whatever she decided on doing, and she was going to do something, she would have to do it alone.

'Good night, Greg,' she said softly. 'And thank you for this evening. It has been one of the——'

The ringing telephone was so startling that they both swung round as if it might at any moment become actually animate.

Julie's movement towards answering was so slight she might not have made it at all. Nearly eleven o'clock. It could only be her mother, who, finding her away from the apartment earlier, had stayed up for a long distance call whose purpose would be no more than to say, 'How are you, darling? I happened to be thinking of you.'

Aching to hear that quick, warm voice, Julie knew that she dare not indulge herself. They had always been close, too close to deceive one another. No matter how hard she tried to prevent it, her voice would give her away, would betray the fact that she was in trouble. A kind of trouble which she must keep from her mother at all costs. That the ghost of personal agony should have been so brutally resurrected for her, was no excuse for the added cruelty of visiting it upon her parents. Insulated, as they were, by distance and the preoccupations of a real metropolis, she prayed that they would never need to know that a fair-haired child called Susie Philips had either lived, or died.

The telephone rang for a long time before it finally fell silent.

'Forgive me,' Julie whispered, and Greg knew that she was not speaking to him.

She turned, and said haltingly, 'That was—probably—probably my mother——' And then she was crying unrestrainedly, her face hidden against his shoulder, her whole body shaken with terrible sobs, while broken words poured forth with the tears she could not check.

What she told him was incoherent, but sufficiently repetitive in its incoherency that he very quickly pieced together a story which explained much about her that he might not otherwise have understood.

'Julie,' he murmured, stroking her hair, 'don't, darling. Don't hurt yourself so much.'

With one, last, shuddering sob, Julie pulled herself away from him. 'I'm so sorry,' she said. 'But thank you. That was building up, I guess. Please don't look at me.

I'll go and make myself look human again. Get yourself a drink. In the left-hand cupboard above the sink.'

'Can I mix one for you, too?'

'No, thank you.'

'You need it. Doctor's orders.'

'You're a bully, like all doctors,' Julie said, and fled to the bathroom.

He went into the kitchen, and quickly located not only an unopened bottle of scotch whisky, but glasses, ice and a tray. These things assembled, he put them on a low table in front of the couch, and lit a cigarette while he waited for her to come back. Knowing what he now did about her, he realized that her control had had to break sooner or later. She was undoubtedly ashamed of her tears, but she would be much better for having shed them.

Strolling up and down the long room, he by-passed an empty easel, and came to a stop in front of a stack of canvases which stood against the wall. Idly, he began to pull them back one after the other, taking his time, reading the compelling history of a single autumn from the first faint gold of early September, through the rich reds of October, to the fast-fading remnants of colour which were all that remained beneath grey November skies.

There was nothing to prepare him for the portrait of Deborah.

Shocked into complete immobility, he stared at a smooth, soulless travesty of a young girl, so skilfully and faithfully portrayed that it made a mockery not only of the subject but of anybody who looked into those witless brown eyes.

Rigid, hypnotized, he did not hear Julie come back into the room; did not even know that she was standing beside him until he heard her say, 'Oh—so you've found that. I shouldn't have left it there.'

'Julie. In the name of God, why did you do it?'

'Horrible, isn't it?' she said steadily.

'Horrible! It's terrifying.'

Blue eyes which still showed signs of her recent tears, searched his face in an effort to read his thoughts. 'You think I'm a ghoul, don't you?'

There was no hesitation in his reply. 'No. I know you're not, and never could be. There must be some rational explanation for this.'

A slight catch in her voice, Julie said, 'You trust me so much. Too much.'

Leaning forward, she reached for another canvas behind the one at which he had been looking, and stood the two, side by side, away from the others.

It was a full minute before Greg spoke again. When he did, he felt that his words were supremely inadequate. 'You've achieved the impossible. You know that, don't you? A hundred years ago they would have burned you for witchcraft.'

'I did it for Clare.'

'Did she know what she was asking of you?'

'Not really.'

'But you did it, anyway.'

'I was so damn sorry for her,' Julie said quietly. 'She didn't realize that I would have to do two complete portraits—before and after. She thought I could build up what she wanted from snapshots and a rough sketch of Deborah for bone structure.'

Looking at the second portrait, the face of a young girl vibrant with beauty and intelligence, Greg saw Deborah as he had seen her for a fractional moment in time, and wished he dared tell Julie that she had accomplished a miracle without a flaw in it.

Julie, with a shrug of distaste, returned both canvases to their original position, face against the wall. 'I can get rid of the first one now. It haunts me. But without it, I couldn't *know* the detail of skin, and bone, and hair as I had to know them to get a convincing portrait. A direct copy of a photograph would have been as lifeless, as unsatisfactory as the photograph itself.'

'Could you have done it in reverse?'

Julie shivered. 'Robbed her of her soul? No. Never.'

He followed her to the couch, and raised his glass in a silent toast to her. There are, he thought, too many threads tying her into this thing. Every facet of it is touching her. So deeply involved emotionally, in such diverse ways, can she remain passive, doing nothing?

And because he was afraid that she neither could nor would, fears he had quieted earlier returned in greater force than before. 'Julie, will you do something for me?'

'That depends on what it is.'

'Will you go home?'

'No, Greg. I'm sorry. I would do a great deal for you, but I won't do that.'

Because she already meant so much to him, and because he was so deadly afraid for her, he was suddenly angry. 'You'll do anything except what I want. Is that it?'

'If that's what you want to think, I can't stop you thinking it.'

'But you don't deny it?'

'Greg—I'm not still on the witness stand, you know.'

'I wish you'd talked yourself into jail while you were,' he told her violently. 'It's the only place where I could be sure you'd be safe from yourself.'

If Julie had not cried, releasing the tension of the previous two days, she would undoubtedly have relieved some of that tension in a real quarrel. As it was, she said pleadingly, 'Please, Greg. You've known me less than twenty-four hours. You can't expect to run my life for me on quite such short notice.'

God, she's lovely, the man thought, and his changing expression reflected what he was thinking.

'That's better,' Julie said, smiling. 'Now, it really is late. You must go. And go quickly so that I can remember you when you're not looking quite so formidable.'

Two minutes later, she stood listening to his car starting on the empty street below, a smile still on her lips. But when the last sound of the motor had died away, she moved purposefully, unsmiling, towards the locked desk drawer where she had hidden a portrait of a murderer as she had seen him while still standing over the body of a small, totally defenceless kill.

X

At midnight on that Thursday night, the ravine was as dark and silent as the valley of death itself. Its thick, black canopy of branches was as motionless as the windless darkness, as secretive as the deep earth trough it shielded.

Unseen, soundless, the sullen pools in the depths of the ravine swelled and spread, bloated by rivulets of rain-water which slithered inexorably down its steep sides: which crept around the boles of the trees: which filtered noiselessly through the lesser resistance of undergrowth obscene with funguses which had never seen the light of day.

Shunned even by the owls, it knew no movement other than this dreary invasion of minute streams which it would eventually absorb with slow reluctance. A reluctance not duplicated by the morbid eagerness with which it took the night into itself and became one with it.

Severed, as if by a will of its own, from all but the powers of darkness, it seemed to brood with deliberate malice upon the evil secrets it guarded: seemed to revel in a black, inanimate triumph belonging only to itself.

Brooding over a dark past, savouring the taste and smell of recent death, the trees and bushes which were its real substance became linked one to another in a tangled threat as ugly as it was positive.

At midnight Deborah moaned once, in a house where the doors always stood open at night.

Clare, although she had been sleeping, was out of bed in an instant. Moving like a wraith, she crossed the hall to a room which she had insisted on keeping unchanged, although none of its adolescent treasures were now in any way suitable to its occupant.

At times she thought that, in sleep, Deborah showed some faint flicker of a lost intelligence. And she clung to a hope she had shared with nobody, that sometime her tall, once beautiful child might, in crossing the borderline between sleeping and waking, cross another borderland.

If this were to happen, it must not happen to her alone.

But whatever the dream which had disturbed Deborah, by the time Clare reached her, the night-light showed a face, even with vacant eyes closed, as blank in its abnormal tranquillity as the pink and white face of a dark-haired doll. A doll which no child would be likely to want.

At midnight, Tom Denning, having looked upon the wine when it was red and not inclined to regret the fact, left Minelli's. After an abortive attempt to get into a car he had never seen before, he located his own. With what he considered to be considerable dignity, he established himself behind the wheel.

Because there was virtually no traffic to consider, he arrived at and negotiated the first corner successfully. Turning the second, he ran across the kerb. At the third, he overcompensated to such a degree that a black Cadillac, parked with its lights out, lost a noticeable amount of expensive paint work. Jamming on his brakes, Denning left his own undamaged convertible in an exposed position in the middle of the road and charted an unsteady course towards the Cadillac.

'Innocent bystander,' he murmured. 'Inebriated news-paperman not so lost of all decency that he will not make amends. Good evening!'

When the fact that the car was empty had penetrated the fumes with which his thinking processes were fogged, he pushed his hat back on his red head, and debated the situation with himself. 'Nobody home? Very odd. Very odd indeed. What now, Denning? Will you admit defeat, or will you outwit the bastard?'

There seemed, at the moment, to be only one pos-sible answer to such a challenge, Pulling a notebook from his hip pocket, he circled the car in order to record its license number.

Tom Denning had never seen any need to waste money on what might be considered a good address. Money was, in his opinion, better spent on more amusing things. His basic requirements included little more than a comfortable bed, and a cupboard large enough to house his two suits, and he paid as little for this accommodation as he possibly could. Since he had, by instinct rather than reason, been headed in the right direction, he was now in what could not by any stretch of the imagination be considered the best part of town.

'Cunning, that's what does it, my boy,' he muttered, leaning down to peer at numbers not easy to read in what was one of the darkest parts of an ill-lit street.

With exaggerated care, he copied the license down without at first finding anything significant in it. 'A doctor? Well, well. Your unprovoked attack on a healer on his rounds is even more despicable than you thought, Denning. Must make note of time and address. No detail to be overlooked, if proof of guilt is to be conclusive.'

Crossing a narrow sidewalk to a brick wall flush with the street, he added another set of figures to the data with which he was, in spite of all imaginary opposition, to stand self-accused. It was not until he had done this that he realized exactly where he was.

Suddenly sobered by the smell of fresh scandal, something fresh air never did for him, he shook his head sharply, and rubbed his hand hard over his forehead and cheeks. Then, eyes narrowed, he looked from a car, too opulent to be in this neighbourhood for professional reasons, to the house outside which it stood. There had recently come to his attention stories about that particular house which he had not yet had time to confirm. The stories had been extremely unpleasant, even to Denning who, if he harboured few scruples, was still a man of normal tastes.

Interesting, he thought. Very interesting, indeed. Perhaps not so innocent a bystander, after all.

Shoving his notebook back into his pocket, he turned quickly on his heel, now in haste to dissociate himself from damages which, in a more characteristic frame of mind, he wondered why he had ever thought of pinning on himself.

He would run that license number down first thing in the morning, and get one of his best men to check at once on the house. It would have to be done with care. When you were handling dynamite, it was always advisable to do so with care.

And this, Tom Denning thought with pleasure, promised to be dynamite.

Mrs. Wylie, who usually went to sleep as soon as her head touched the pillow, got up at midnight more wide awake than when she had gone to bed two hours earlier.

A small, white-haired marquise in yellow quilted satin, she went into her living-room, opened a drawer in a mahogany desk, and took out the lease for her apartment. Quickly scanning fine print, she found that her memory had not been at fault. If she gave notice at once, she would be free to leave at the end of the year.

Slowly she walked through the three rooms she had furnished with such care, noticing every detail of a place in which she had thought she would stay until she died. A place she had taken five years earlier, not only for the convenience of its location, but for its superb view across the green sea of the ravine.

I don't know where I'll go, she thought bleakly, but I cannot stay here. My leisure hours are too few and too precious to be maimed by so constant a reminder of so much I would forget if only I could. That girl, Julie Warner, was too graphic in what she said. Before I heard her today, I had no definite picture in my mind. Now I am condemned to see Deborah struggling in a dark hell more awful than anything I have imagined myself. From now on, to look out of my windows here will be to see the blackest night even at high noon, to see evil forever stalking innocence through the underbrush of a jungle from which there is no escape.

Beating one tiny fist against the other, she thought, why didn't they listen to her, that girl who tried to tell them what they would not see as truth! Why doesn't somebody do something, quickly, quickly, before it happens again! And why do I think that I, more perhaps than any other, have some definite reason for crediting the existence of a man who really does, at times at least, resemble the Devil himself? I am as bad as Clare with her second sight. And as pathetically helpless.

Abruptly she tightened a yellow satin belt, as if by doing so she tightened a self-control which rarely ever threatened to desert her as it did then. I'll get myself something to eat, she told herself firmly, and then I'll go back to bed.

In a gleaming kitchenette, she set about preparing cocoa, her movements precise and efficient. When this was done, she took out bread and part of a cold ham. She had cut the bread, put the knife away, and picked up a carving knife, when her hand suddenly faltered, and her eyes became fixed on a long, shining blade honed to razor sharpness.

The harsh clatter of the knife as it struck the tiled floor was far less shocking to Mrs. Wylie than the instant of revelation which had shown her to herself as potentially able, if given sufficient cause, to kill another human being.

Murder, Captain Velyan thought sombrely, is nearly always a harsh, unheralded disturbance of a comparatively placid pond: an ugly, misshapen pebble which cannot help but leave ever-widening ripples behind it. Yet his presence in his office at midnight was, he knew, proof that in this case the ripples were vanishing with their cause, leaving not a trace behind them.

With an angry gesture, he thrust aside a sheaf of reports which, although they represented hours of careful police work, told nothing of any value at all.

Brilliant, unhappy eyes deep sunk in a face lined with fatigue, he thought, it's the Hurst case all over again. Plaster casts of footprints, blurred by soft mud, which are utterly useless. An inch by inch examination of every single footpath into the ravine, yielding nothing, any clue there might have been washed away by seepage which in this weather never ceases. Was it accident which had produced the same weather conditions in both cases? It seemed highly unlikely. And neither on the victim, nor in the trampled mud, any tangible evidence which could be used except in relation to a definite suspect. Nothing but some soft fuzz from a heavy, dark material such as might be used in making a man's coat. Even given a suspect with a coat of that material, could he be condemned on such flimsy evidence? Condemned beyond a reasonable doubt? No. It needed more than that. Much more than that. It needed finger-prints. And the man had, according to medical evidence, worn gloves: gloves of some very thin substance, thin but tough: probably rubber. More than anything, it needed an eye witness who could recognize, and testify, without equivocation, without imagination. He did not doubt for a minute that Julie Warner honestly thought she had seen what she said she had seen. What he could not believe was that she had really seen a man such as she had described. She might, unknown to herself, be in possession of more specific knowledge than she had so far admitted to, but after the evidence she had given in court that day, anything further she might add at a later date could be ridiculed to nothing by any first year law student. A courageous girl, certainly, and a very attractive one, but a useless witness.

The District Attorney's office had been unpleasant enough when he had failed in the Hurst affair. They were going to raise hell if he didn't break this one.

This should have been a major consideration with him, but it counted for little beside his own burning, personal need to see justice done. If he failed again, he intended to turn in his badge without being asked.

His gaze fixed on a bare expanse of wall in need of painting, he knew that his best lead to date was Gregory Markham's assertion that both girls had been violated by the same man, and that he was a man who knew exactly how to strangle with the greatest possible hope of success. He had followed this up in the only way which had so far occurred to him, and had got in touch with Washington in an effort to find out how many of the town's permanent residents had taken commando training. It was a line which would be doggedly plugged at, but he was convinced in advance that it would lead nowhere. Instinct told him that the answer, if he ever found it, would be less ordinary than that. And though he knew that instinct could be fallible, in this instance he did not believe that it was.

If only there were some specific line of action which could be taken, he thought bitterly. Anything, as long as it was action, no matter how slim the hope.

I should go home, he told himself. I'm doing no damn good to anyone, sitting here. And thinking of home, he thought of his child, a girl, not quite three years old, who would probably be dark later on, but who still retained a baby fairness. Before he could prevent it, a single, violent oath was wrung from him, as an image of other fair curls matted with mud superimposed itself on his mental picture of his own daughter.

Greg, knowing he needed sleep, had intended to go straight back to the hospital residence after leaving Julie. Instead, at midnight, he was in his office giving his complete and frowning attention to a page of notes gleaned from three different books on psychiatry.

It's just possible that it could be brought off, he thought, but dare I risk it?

Leaning back, long fingers reaching absently for a cigarette, he considered a calculated risk which would necessitate stopwatch timing, and the co-operation of three women, two of whom would have to be exposed to totally dissimilar forms of danger.

And as he studied the possibility which had been forming in the back of his mind all day, he realized that he was thinking of Deborah not as she was, but as she should have been, more woman than child.

Julie, in blue striped pyjamas, her feet tucked up under her, sat in a corner of the couch at midnight, a drawing-board on her lap, a devil in black and white glaring down at her from her easel.

In planning a definite, independent line of action,

she knew that she was asking for every possible kind of trouble, not the least to her being Greg's anger. She had been sufficiently driven by her own crying need to do something, without the goad provided by Barbara's visit. Now she was compelled by a force stronger than fear, more powerful even than past pity and grief. If there were to be another, it was a thousand to one against its being Barbara, but Barbara was her living, breathing symbol of the unknown child she must save if it lay within her power to do so.

Her pencil poised, the terrible isolation of her undertaking struck her with real force. Needing the people who loved her as she was unlikely ever to need them again, she was cut off from them simply because they loved her, because, if she allowed it, they would prevent her from doing what she was so grimly determined to do.

Starting to draw again, she considered, as she worked, how she could approach Captain Velyan and Tom Denning, both of whom must be persuaded to co-operate with her. It seemed to her that her best chance of selling her idea lay in seeing them together. Denning would probably be the less difficult of the two. The front page of Friday's *Courier*, as she envisaged it, was a lay-out which should tempt any newspaperman. A two-inch headline, and below that her own picture flanked by four sketches, the first of which was giving her more trouble than she had anticipated.

In theory, it had seemed easy to draw four satanic faces, all of them entirely different, no one of them bearing any real resemblance to the original on the easel. But, do what she would, the likeness would creep in. It was like holding a pencil at a séance, and having it move apparently of its own volition.

'The devil!' she exclaimed, and was unamused by her unintentional irony, as she tore up what she had done, and began all over again.

Barbara, waking at midnight, did not know what

time it was, or why she should have waked at all. Listening sleepily for any sound in the quiet of the big, dark house, and hearing none, she rolled herself up in a small, comfortable ball, and pulled the blankets over her head. But, as soon as she had done this, she realized what had been bothering her. She had forgotten to say her prayers. This was not unusual, and normally she would have fallen back on a highly personal arrangement with God to say them twice the following night. God, fortunately, was not nearly as fussy as her mother was about such things.

Tonight, however, was different, because it marked a change in a ritual which had been unchanged as far back as she could remember. To wait until tomorrow to make this change would, she knew, be wrong.

Shivering a little, she crawled out of the blankets and slid over the edge of the bed on to her knees.

'Our Father Which art in Heaven——'

It was the same as it had always been until she came to the moment when she was accustomed to asking that Susie be looked after.

I will not cry, she told herself sturdily. You don't ask God to look after people who are already in heaven, and you don't cry about them. God would probably be even more annoyed than Mummy if I cried because Susie was in heaven. It would be a very impolite thing to do.

Her soft whisper clear and unhesitating, she made the change which meant that at least there would be no gap in the number of people for whom she prayed.

'—and please look after Miss Warner, too.'

XI

On Friday morning, Julie, who had gone to bed at four, got up at eight-thirty and immediately called the police station.

'Captain Velyan, please. Miss Warner calling.'

Velyan's weariness carried even over the telephone. 'Hello, Miss Warner?'

'May I see you this morning? It's quite important.'

'I'm tied up until ten, or a little after. Would ten-thirty be time enough?'

'Yes,' Julie told him. 'Thank you. I would like to bring Mr. Denning of the *Courier* with me, if I may.'

The police captain's tone was less non-committal than his words. 'Are you sure that's advisable.'

'Not only advisable, but necessary.'

'I leave it to your judgement, but I would suggest that you think it over first. There's a limit to what can be kept off-the-record with the Press, simply by asking.'

'What I have to say I want on-the-record,' Julie told him quietly. 'My hope is that you will agree with me.'

Before calling the *Courier* office she went to the kitchen and made a pot of strong coffee, and, knowing she should eat, toasted two slices of bread. While the coffee was percolating, she walked through a connecting door into the bathroom and splashed cold water on a face which in the grey morning light reminded her of faces she had seen on the Riviera. Thank God I have a photograph to give them, she thought wryly. If they took one today they could be forgiven for mixing it up with one of my own damnable drawings.

Still in her pyjamas, she carried a tray into the studio. She put the tray down, and pulled back curtains which it would have been an admission of weakness to have left closed. Looking out over the ravine, she wondered if it would seem less hostile in sunlight, and decided that it would not. With the sun on it, it would now remind her of a bog thinly disguised by bright scum.

Tom Denning, when Julie's call was put through to him, was whistling softly through his teeth while he took in the implications of the name he had just learned was that of a black Cadillac's owner. Reaching slowly for his telephone, he realized that to play with dynamite would be a relatively harmless performance when compared with tying this name to a house of more than ill-repute. The *Courier* had yet to face a libel suit since he had been its managing editor, and he had no intention of marring this careful rather than praise-worthy record.

Take pause, Denning, he told himself. No rushing in where the *Sentinel* would fear to tread until you've had time in which to think this thing over. 'Hello. Denning here.'

'Julie Warner, Mr. Denning. Have you some free time this morning?'

To anyone else at that moment Tom Denning would have said no, he had not, and would probably have followed this up with a query as to whether his listener thought newspapers were hatched out of eggs.

'Miss Warner? How are you? Yes, I might be able to manage something.'

'What is your usual deadline?' Julie asked.

Tom Denning did some fast thinking. This call might be based on nothing more than a false alarm. On the other hand it might not. He would, he decided, lose nothing by playing along until he found out what it was all about.

'One o'clock is our usual deadline, Miss Warner. For an exclusive that we think worth the trouble we can stretch that a bit.'

'What I have for you is exclusive, and I think you'll decide it's worth some trouble.'

'Can you give me any idea of what it's all about?'

'No,' Julie told him decisively. 'I want Captain Velyan to hear what I have to say at the same time that you do. I have an appointment with him for ten-thirty. Could you meet me there?'

'How long will this take?'

'I don't know. That depends in part on you.'

Frowning, Denning thought, I asked for it, and I've got it. 'I'll be there,' he said.

Julie's hesitation was brief. 'It would be better if we didn't arrive together. It might even be a good idea if you could manage to go in by some back entrance, if there is one.'

Well, well, Denning thought to himself. This gets curiouser and curiouser. This is, I believe, Denning, the first time that a lady has ever invited you into a police station by the back door. Your virtue, at least, is unlikely to be put to the test. 'Whatever you say, Miss Warner. This seems to be your party.'

My party, Julie thought grimly, as she put down the telephone. My party, and time to go put on my false face since I intend to direct the fun and games.

She poured herself a third cup of coffee, and lit one cigarette from the end of another. Then she made up the couch bed, and started to get ready to go out. She chose a plain grey suit and a tailored white blouse. In making this choice, she was doing what she could to play down the effect of her blonde hair, something in a woman which she had found made it difficult for men to take her seriously.

And these men must be made to take her seriously.

Ready too soon, unable to sit quietly, she opened the door at the top of the stairs, and looked down to see if there was any mail lying on the floor inside the outer door. Expecting, at most, to see one or two letters, and perhaps a circular, she could not credit the evidence of her own eyes. How very odd, she thought, and then immediately recognized the fact that the only oddity lay in her own lack of mental preparedness for this.

Her face inscrutable, she descended the stairs, gathered up more than twenty letters of all sizes and shapes, and carried them back to the studio.

As she had known they would be, they were nearly all crank letters, some of them so unpleasant they made her feel tainted with the smallness of mind and spirit which had dictated their contents. I have made myself notorious, she thought. It was a thought which made her sick. She took all but two letters to the kitchen sink where she burned them, while trying to pretend that it was the acrid smoke which made her eyes sting.

The two she had kept were some recompense for the others.

Susie's father had written '…will never forget what you did. We can never thank you enough. My wife has asked me to give you her love….'

And Mrs. Grey, whom she had not met, had said, 'What you did for Barbara yesterday is something nobody else could have done. You must know how grateful I am. She is herself again. Will you have dinner with us next week? Please say you will, and choose the night which suits you best.'

Tomorrow, Julie thought, there will be more like those I burned. I'll get Greg to sort my mail for me—that is if we are still on speaking terms by tomorrow. Putting on her coat, and picking up her portfolio, she was not at all sure that this would be the case.

It was a twenty-minute walk from her apartment to the police station behind the courthouse, and Julie, with minutes still to put in, decided to leave the station-wagon and follow the road around the ravine on foot. Deliberately crossing the street to the ravine side, she tried to rationalize a repulsion which her mind insisted was irrational. She looked up at the tops of pines mixed with elms and maples by contrast more stark and skeletal than if they had stood alone, and tried to see them as trees no different from trees anywhere: a natural growth, quiescent, inactive now until another spring. Yet, even as she watched, a gusty wind brought murmuring movement to heavy masses of needles so dark a green they appeared almost black, caused bare branches to rattle against one another with an angry melancholy which seemed to hunger for the death of all things as yet spared by the harsh breath of winter. And in the sodden, withered carpet of dead leaves from which the trees sprang, the edge of the same wind plucked into motion small furtive shapes which rose, fell back, and rose again as if in an effort to clutch at and drag down any living creature which trespassed near them.

That this should be only the outer fringe of a gorge, in whose depths a murky twilight passed as day, increased rather than decreased an insensate threat against which reason had no effective weapon. If a place could in itself be evil, then this was such a place: a dark, and ever-present invitation to hidden violence which, without that invitation, might find itself thwarted. Perversion and brutality, she knew, might exist anywhere. Here the ravine stood accessory to these things in that it provided opti-mum conditions for their unrevenged outlet.

The closer she drew to the courthouse square the more acutely she became aware of a school holiday which did not owe its origin to a normal calendar freedom. Streets which, at mid-morning, were usually sparsely filled with housewives, delivery men, and old people, today were roamed by groups of children of all ages up to thirteen and fourteen. Children who, having no fixed objective, showed little or no evidence of the high spirits with which they would have greeted an escape they had been able to plan for in advance. Some, but not all, were troubled by Susie's ghost. The majority, though probably unaware of this, were simply frustrated by a break in their routine which had caught them unprepared.

An uneasy cluster of teenagers, idling outside the central post office, stared at her as she approached, and, she was quite certain, continued to stare after she had passed them. And why not, she thought bitterly. It's not everyone who is privileged enough to see someone who claims to have seen the Devil himself. She tried not to mind the stares she received, but she minded very much. And though she considered the police station dreary beyond description, she was relieved when she reached it.

Captain Velyan received her with a courtesy oddly out of place in the unadorned severity of his office.

She was scarcely seated in the chair he had drawn forward for her, when Tom Denning came in.

Denning, his expression quizzical, said, "'And when shall we three meet again? In thunder, lightening, or in rain?" What's cooking, my fellow witches, or hasn't the brew of snakes-livers and toadstools started to simmer yet?'

If he insists on being flippant, Julie thought, I'm going to have a hard time with this. But she had to bite her lip to keep from smiling. For, looked at objectively, as he had made her do, they were in truth an odd trio.

'Miss Warner has just arrived,' Velyan said pleasantly. 'Sit down, Denning, and we won't need to waste any time.'

'I stand rebuked. United I stand—together we sit.' He swung a chair around from its original position, and straddled it, his arms crossed along its back.

Julie, meeting the gaze of probing hazel eyes, recognized the cleverness of a manoeuvre which, without emphasis, put the newspaperman where he could best watch both herself and the police captain.

In the silence which fell then, she experienced a moment of panic in which she wondered if she were capable of presenting herself and her idea with the necessary conviction.

Velyan, almost too sensitive to the feelings of others, at once put her at her ease again. 'It's obvious at this time that we have only one really compelling interest in common. I don't imagine I'm wrong, Miss Warner, in thinking that you wish to see us in connection with Susan Philips' death.'

His quiet voice gave dignity to the concept of death, even in the form in which it had overtaken Susie. And Julie added gratitude to her original liking for him. Even if he did not think much of her idea, at least he would not ridicule it.

'You're quite right,' she said. 'But before I say anything more, I must tell you one or two things about myself. This is necessary because you must see me in a somewhat different light from that in which I was seen at the inquest yesterday. And also because you must fully understand what this thing means to me. You see, I—I had a young sister who died in much the same way Susie Philips died. That was five years ago. But one doesn't forget easily.'

Velyan thought, she should have told me this before. It explains the swiftness of the action she took, increases her reliability as an individual. 'Would you like to smoke?' he asked.

'Thank you. I would.'

Denning, without speaking, held out a battered silver cigarette case, and gave her a light.

'Now,' Julie said, and she spoke with clear confidence.

'I want you to see me as an expert in my own field. Verbally I can be confused, and driven into an untenable position, like anybody else. With a pencil in my hand, I am never either confused or uncertain. I am a trained observer who, in my own medium, would find it difficult, if not impossible, to misrepresent anything I really looked at. I am, at the moment, for reasons of my own, a public school teacher. If you can, will you forget that, and concentrate on the fact that I have already had two very successful exhibitions of paintings in New York, and prior to that six years of the best instruction that money can buy, both here and abroad. I don't like underlining my own competence in this way, but unless you accept me as fully competent I'll be wasting both my time and yours.'

Looking from one man to the other, she could see that she had impressed them by her manner, if nothing else.

She touched the portfolio at her side, and continued. 'I have some drawings here which I am going to show you in a minute. One of them is a portrait of a spoken description which, to put it mildly, was unconvincing. I only saw the man it represents for perhaps a quarter of a second, but that is infinitely longer than fliers are given for specific aircraft identification on a screen. Five minutes would have given me no clearer impression, or one that was any more detailed.'

Dear God, I hope I am doing this properly, she prayed. I sound to myself like a visiting lecturer.

Her hands not quite steady, she opened her portfolio and drew out her devil and laid it silently on Velyan's desk.

Rising, Tom Denning went around behind the police captain to look at it. He whistled softly. 'Nasty customer, isn't he?'

Velyan, his long, unhappy face betraying no reaction, looked at the malignant mark, glanced for an instant at

Julie, and looked down again. Julie, through the long watches of two nights had thought over every word Greg had said about a facsimile of this drawing, and had arrived at what were some very astute conclusions. She now proceeded to state them as if they were facts.

'I saw that face, exactly as you see it now. Yet I know, as well as anyone else would, that it does not exist exactly as you see it. A trick of the light, combined with an inhuman expression, has disguised that face as effectively as hours of laborious make-up might not have done. But there are two features—the nose and the mouth—which are probably, I think undoubtedly, those of the man himself, undistorted and true in every detail. Now look——'

She placed a square of cardboard, with an oblong hole cut in it, over the drawing, so that only the nose and mouth were left. 'Do you see what I mean?'

'By these things shall ye know him——' Denning murmured softly. 'By heaven, Miss Warner, you've sold me. Where do we go from here?'

'Captain Velyan?' Julie queried.

His brilliant eyes locking with hers, Velyan said quietly, 'This is knowledge, Miss Warner, which could be very dangerous to you, without being of sufficient use to me. Even if we were to find a man, among thousands, with this nose and mouth, and they are both distinctive, he could not be convicted of murder on the strength of that alone.'

I'm going to win, Julie thought, and thrust from her the further correlative that in winning she might lose.

'I think I get your idea, Miss Warner,' Denning said, speaking rapidly. 'We publish this picture, and beside it a cut of the nose and mouth, and ask the public to hunt him down. Jesus Murphy, what a lovely spread I can make of that!'

'No!' Julie said sharply. 'That isn't my idea at all. I don't want this—this animal on the run, never to be caught. I want to go to bed at night knowing that he will never be able to do again what he has done twice already.'

Startled by her vehemence, Denning scratched his head, and said, 'Then what's the pitch, first witch? I don't get it.'

Julie reached into the portfolio again and took out four more drawings, smaller but no less clear than the first, and spread them out in front of the two men.

'Here are four more devils,' she said, 'all with quite possible noses and mouths. I want you, Mr. Denning, to put them in your paper as the work of your own staff artist. You set them up, two on either side of a picture of myself which I have here, and headline it something to this effect—CAN ARTIST DRAW RAVINE DEVIL? Then below, you outline a hypothetical interview with myself in which I am induced to make a drawing for Saturday's *Courier*. You then go on with my qualifications as an artist. Beaux Arts, New York School of Fine Art, and so on. You add to that a strong vote of confidence from the *Courier*, itself. All your readers will lap it up, whether they believe I can do it or not. But one reader—I hope—will be afraid not to believe: will stop me, if he can, between the time the *Courier* goes on to the streets this afternoon and, I would guess, tomorrow morning.'

'I'd take my hat off to you, witch, if I had it on,' Denning said casually. 'You've got guts. Give me the print of your own pretty phiz, and I'll get on with my part of the show, pronto.'

'Just a minute, Denning,' Velyan said incisively. 'You may think a headline is a fair return for Miss Warner's life, but I don't.'

'You'll look after her,' Denning replied easily.

'And if I can't?'

An even bigger headline, Tom Denning thought, before he could stop himself. Aloud, he said, 'This is Miss Warner's idea, not mine, I might remind you, Captain.'

'And I haven't bought her idea.'

Julie spoke to Velyan as if he and she were alone. 'But you will, won't you? Because you and I both want the same thing for the same reasons. Because we neither of us, being the people we are, can refuse to try anything which might possibly accomplish the purpose we share.'

Velyan, too well aware of the dead end which the police faced in an investigation already a failure, still could not accept a proposal which included so much more than a possibility of serious harm to the girl who made it.

Julie, appreciating his dilemma, made the decision for him.

She picked up the four sketches, added her own photograph to them, and placed them in Tom Denning's willing hands. 'You have my authority, Mr. Denning, to use these pictures in the manner which has just been discussed. Captain Velyan is not, I'm afraid, in a position to interfere, much as he would like to. In as far as you can make the two compatible, will you present me as a good artist but at the same time a high-strung, not too bright bohemian?'

'No collusion with intelligent young woman, police lurking in the background, to be suspected?'

He's a louse, Julie thought, but I can see why Greg likes him. 'My idea precisely.'

'If it t'were done, t'were well t'were done properly. You can count on me. You will be a Little Red Riding Hood as gullible as you are beautiful.'

As soon as he had said it, Denning knew that he could have chosen a happier metaphor. Feeling that apology, towards which he was disinclined anyway, would not improve matters, he moved towards the door. But before actually leaving, he said, 'The boy-friend know anything about this stunt, Miss Warner?'

He means Greg. 'No.'

'I thought not. If he did, you wouldn't be here. See you nice people around.'

When the door had closed behind him, Julie looked levelly at a man in whose keeping she felt her life would be safer than in most. 'I'm sorry to have been so high-handed, Captain Velyan.'

'In doing yourself no favour, you do me one.'

'I know,' she said. And added, with a quiet smile, '"A policeman's lot is not a happy one." Mr. Denning's habit of quotation and mis-quotation seems to be catching.'

'Have you thought this thing through at all, Miss Warner?'

'Not much further than this,' Julie admitted. 'If I had, I might not have been able to do it at all.'

'Would it be taken as an impertinence if I asked who the friend was to whom Denning referred? Anything at all important to you is now of some importance to me.'

Swiftly Julie considered whether or not she should tell him the truth about herself and Greg, and how they had met. Deciding that to do so would be to betray a confidence unnecessarily, she confined herself to the simplest answer possible. 'Dr. Gregory Markham.'

'Oh. He was a friend of mine. Or I liked to think so.' 'Was?'

'He won't be after this. He will, from what I know of him, be ready to cut the heart out of anyone who has had anything to do with it.'

'Including me,' Julie told him in a small voice.

Velyan's rare smile briefly lightened his expression. 'I doubt that.'

'You think my idea might work?' Julie asked, almost hoping he would deny the possibility.

'Yes,' Velyan told her. 'I do. In my job, even when one has very little to go on, one forms a remarkably definite impression of any unknown man, or woman, who has committed murder. It is in part intuition, in part memory of other crimes and the people who perpetrated them, and in part the killing itself. In this particular case, I feel that we are dealing with a man who is not only clever but intelligent, and who wants at all costs to keep his place in this town. I'll go further, and say that my guess is that this is a place well worth keeping. So much so, that he may cease to be clever in his attempt to retain it.'

'I have felt that, too,' Julie said, and chill fingers seemed to brush across the back of her neck. 'If he were just a tramp——'

'You would have liked it better. Or, I should say, disliked it less.'

'Yes. It would have been less—corrupt.'

The chill which had touched her seemed to communicate itself to Velyan. With a quick gesture of exasperation, he became entirely practical. 'I take it that you don't want to be killed, Miss Warner?'

'I never wanted anything as little.'

'Then you will follow these instructions to the letter. From this moment on, you will neither run, nor move suddenly, at any time. One of my best men will be following you when you leave here, and he must not, for any reason, lose sight of you before he sees you safely inside your own door. Don't be tempted to look behind you. He will be there, I promise you. There will also be a radio patrol car which will be keeping in touch with me.'

'Isn't this all a bit unnecessary until the *Courier* comes out?' Julie protested.

'Think, Miss Warner!'

'Oh,' Julie said flatly. 'You're thinking of the *Courier*'s staff.'

'I am thinking that from the moment Tom Denning took those drawings out of this office anything could happen. Now, I don't want you to use your car again until after dark. From dusk onwards, there will be one of my men hidden in it. And from dusk onwards, don't go anywhere *except* in your car. Next, don't make any calls on your telephone, and if friends call you, get rid of them at

127

once. Make any excuse you like, but keep that line clear. Next, keep your door locked.'

'But shouldn't I go out?' Julie asked. 'If I shut myself up in the apartment, with someone on guard outside, I'll be too safe.'

Velyan beat a light tattoo on the edge of his desk before speaking again. Then he said slowly, 'I think that once it starts to get dark, that is exactly what you should do. If you were really working on a drawing for tomorrow's *Courier*, that is where you would be. And it means that if our man makes any move, he will have to take the initiative. This will give you some warning, give you a better chance.'

'You think it will be the telephone?'

'It will almost have to be. He could come to you. He would be much safer, himself, if he could persuade you to come to him. My guess is that he will try it that way first. So if you receive a call from anyone, asking you to go out for any reason, no matter how ordinary—or, for that matter, how far-fetched—you will agree to go. But on no account go anywhere after dark except in your car.'

'All right,' Julie said, and rising, found her knees not quite as steady as they should have been. 'I imagine that's all, isn't it?'

'Wait a moment.' He picked up his own telephone, gave some decisive orders, listened to the reply, and then hung up.

Walking to the door with her, he said, 'Will you give me your word of honour on one point, Miss Warner?'

'What is that, Captain Velyan?'

'That you will let *nobody* inside your door. That's the one place where you'll have no protection at all.'

'I give you my word.'

'And you won't forget any of the other things I've told you?'

'I'm more likely to forget my own name,' Julie told him with a conviction he found reassuring. 'There are

128

two heavy rugs in the back of the station-wagon which should provide some camouflage for the detective. And I'll have your number beside my telephone. Do you want me to call you if—if I think he has made a move?'

'Use your own judgement on that. If it's a matter of leaving your apartment, I'll know about it in a matter of seconds. At no time will I be out of this building between now and tomorrow morning. So, if it's a question of going out, I foresee no reason for you to call me. If my guess is wrong, and he comes directly to you—then I doubt if your telephone will still be working. In that case, get to your kitchen window and scream. Really scream, Miss Warner.'

Julie took a last look at a bare room whose stark, utilitarian order was strangely comforting.

'*Au revoir*,' she said, holding out her hand.

His clasp was firm and strong, and he followed her lead, his accent surprisingly good. '*Au revoir*, Miss Warner.'

Traversing the windy expanse of the square, on impulse Julie stopped and bought a handful of dried corn from the old woman at the news-stand in the middle of the car park. Scattering it amongst the pigeons which descended on her like a living cloud, she thought sombrely—a superstitious offering, but on whose altar? Then, turning up the collar of her coat against the wind, she turned north along the east side of the ravine. But this time she stayed on the inhabited side of the street.

Passing neat houses in neat gardens, and blocks of small well-kept shops, the water tower a landmark half a mile ahead of her, she felt as if she were talking through an uneasy dream in which these things no longer had any meaning for her. Even the people were puppets, their covert interest in her no longer capable of touching her in any way. Only the ravine was real, and a police detective without a name or a face who, incredibly, was even now following her. The temptation to look back, to try and place him, was almost overwhelming.

This can't be happening to me, she thought. It can't. But it is. And because she so badly needed to re-establish an ordinary contact with everyday normalcy, she did something she had no intention of doing, and turned into the drugstore.

There were a half-dozen people there, scattered between the prescription counter and the magazine rack, most of whom she knew either by sight or to speak to casually. There must have been something in her face to discourage immediate, direct curiosity, because none of them did more than greet her.

Rosie, on the other hand, as Julie slid on to a stool at the fountain, was either too simple or too elated to exercise tact.

She leaned forward across the counter, and said in a stage whisper, 'Did you really see the Devil, Miss Warner, like it says in the paper?'

Aware of a quite unnatural silence behind her, Julie replied evenly, 'More or less.'

'And did he really look like the Devil?'

'He didn't look like the Angel Gabriel. Coffee, Rosie, if you please, and cheese on rye.'

Rosie, her round cheeks rounder than ever, said, 'It's a wonder to me you didn't just drop dead, Miss Warner. What I mean to say is, just seeing him like that would have been enough, I should think.'

The Evil Eye, Julie thought, stifling an hysterical desire to laugh. If I stay in this town, will I ever be able to live this down?

She was to wonder this again when she went into the small grocery and meat store two blocks back from the ravine, where she was in the habit of buying the food she cooked herself.

The dour Scotsman, who owned the store, said nothing until he had wrapped up her purchases for her. Then, his bony face solemn, he said, 'I'm thinking, lass, that a visit to the kirk would be doing ye no harm.'

Julie was no longer in any frame of mind to find what was, in effect, an accusation of heresy, even faintly amusing. 'And I'm thinking, Mr. McNair, that it would do me no harm if the people in this town were to mind their own business. Good morning.'

I shouldn't have done that, she thought, as she came out on to the street, but I would do it again. Stooping to disentangle her feet from muddied pieces of newsprint which had blown against them, she saw her own name in black capitals. 'And again, and again, and again!' she said through her teeth, as she kicked the tattered fragment furiously into the gutter.

When she turned in the direction not only of her apartment, but also of the ravine, she would have broken into a run if she had not remembered that this was one of the things she must no longer do.

XII

Greg, who had hoped to have lunch with Julie, suffered more than a personal disappointment when he called her apartment at noon and received no answer. He would not be free to call again until the early evening, and he had an imperative reason for wanting to talk to her as soon as possible. With every passing hour, his uneasiness on her account had grown. Because of this, he had decided that a calculated risk would be far less dangerous than a nebulous threat that could strike at her with little or no warning. The decision once taken, he wanted to act upon it without delay.

Dismissing as ridiculous an inclination to go out and search the town for her, he knew that he would accomplish more, and faster, by using his time to enlist the help of Clare and Mrs. Wylie. Briefly he wondered if he was wrong in crediting Clare with the self-control she would have to have if she were to be of use as she must be of use. But he saw that if he were to doubt his own judgement in any respect at this juncture, it would be to judge himself unfit to spring the trap he had devised.

Knowing that he just had time to catch Mrs. Wylie before she went out to lunch, he left his office and walked swiftly to the elevators. On several occasions, he had given her a lift at lunchtime, and on this occasion the offer must be as casual as it had been in the past.

There was no perceptible break or hesitation in his stride as he crossed the main lobby downstairs, but he was aware that every muscle in his body had tightened with his recognition of the man already standing easily beside Mrs. Wylie's desk.

'Hello, Bartell,' he said evenly. 'Can I give you a ride, Mrs. Wylie?'

'Thank you, Dr. Markham,' Mrs. Wylie said promptly.

Dr. Bartell's voice was deep and soft, and though his expression was as suave as the smooth, suave voice, black eyes glittered watchfully beneath colourless eyebrows. 'I can take Mrs. Wylie. I am going her way, as it happens.'

To Greg it was as if they were three pieces in a chess game laid out on a gigantic board of black and white tiled squares. A game in which there could be no retreat from a single wrong move, or the suggestion of one. To look, even fleetingly, at Dr. Bartell's powerful, well-manicured hands, would be enough to constitute such a wrong move.

His own hands as steady as they might have been in the middle of a delicate operation, Greg lit a cigarette. 'A black Cadillac, or a blue Buick? Your decision, Mrs. Wylie.'

Mrs. Wylie's small smile did not reach her eyes. 'If Dr. Bartell will forgive me, I'll accept the Buick. I'm not going home today. I'm going to my sister's, and I believe Dr. Markham is going in that direction.'

With a formal inclination of his sleek, dark head, Dr. Bartell said, 'Then I leave you in good hands.'

As he turned away from them, his white silk scarf was blotted from sight, and the slim elegance of his black-clad figure seemed to elongate, so that the impression created by his receding back was that of a very tall man.

'Exit a Black King,' Mrs. Wylie murmured, and there was an unusual edge to her well-bred voice.

Thought transference, Greg asked himself? Or simply a coincidence. Aloud, he said, without appearing to attach any importance to the question, 'You don't like him?'

'No. When I think of Christ on the mountain top being tempted, I always see Dr. Bartell beside——' Her voice died away, the sentence unfinished, but her eyes continued to say what she was suddenly quite incapable of saying in words.

The revolving doors, at the entrance to the lobby, turned as three people came through them. Three ordinary people who had no real place on the chess board, and who would remain forever in ignorance that they had passed across it.

Released from tension too acute for such an exposed place, Mrs. Wylie made a mechanical gesture towards the girls at the switchboard to indicate that she was leaving, and in silence preceded Greg across the lobby to the private entrance.

It was not until the car had left the hospital grounds that either of them spoke again.

Without preface, Mrs. Wylie said, 'Tell me, Dr. Markham, am I going mad?'

Somewhere, sometime, probably a long time ago, Greg though, she has had a glimpse of that face looking a little as Julie saw it. As I saw it. Tonight, tomorrow, next week—she will pin that memory down for her own satisfaction. This isn't a necessity because actually she already knows, had almost certainly known subconsciously for long enough that it is not as great a shock to her conscious mind as it might have been. I do not need to prepare her. She has prepared herself.

'No,' he said. 'You are not mad.'

The sharp intake of her breath was like a piece of cloth ripping, but when she spoke the surgeon knew that he had been right in his assessment.

'You're going to do something?'

'Yes,' he told her.

'You'll let me help?'

'Yes. But both you and your sister will have to agree first to a risk which you may decide is unjustified.'

'I would give my life,' Mrs. Wylie said, and meant it.

'The real risk will not be to you—or to Clare.'

'Oh, no!'

'Yes,' Greg told her quietly. 'Deborah.'

Traffic lights ahead flickered through orange to red. As the car stopped at the pedestrian crossing, he laid his hand firmly over both of hers, where they lay, small, white-gloved, tightly knotted together in her lap. 'Don't talk now. Don't even think, if you can help it. We'll talk when we get to Clare's, and then you and she can help each other to reach any decision you make.'

'Which means that we'll do anything you ask,' Mrs. Wylie said without heat.

Pressing his foot on the accelerator again, Greg said, 'Not necessarily.'

'Yes. I know, because I know Clare. She will do anything you suggest, no matter what it is. Her belief in you is absolute.'

'And yours?'

'Wherever you and Clare lead, I'll follow. But I wish with all my heart that Deborah did not need to be involved.'

Drawing up outside the white bungalow which was their destination, seeing a tall young figure, awkward as a marionette, sidling up the path to the front door, Greg said more than he had intended to say just then. 'You may not continue to regret her involvement. God willing, you may even be glad of it in the long run.'

XIII

At two o'clock, while Greg perforce shut his mind to everything but the difficult operation he was then scheduled to perform, and Julie on the opposite side of the ravine climbed the stairs to her apartment with her groceries, Tom Denning studied the first run of a front page he had laid out himself.

Looking at ink patterns not yet dry, he would have rubbed his hands together if that had been a gesture natural to him. As it was, he whistled tonelessly under his breath, his expression more than self-satisfied.

A beautiful, beautiful job, Denning, he told himself. Something to be proud of, to frame and show to your bastard children even unto the third and fourth generation of the little dears. Now if you were a murderer, Denning, would you bite on this so sweetly baited hook? Would you believe that this pretty chick was as touchingly brainless as she is herein represented to be? Yes, I think you very well might.

The picture of herself which Julie had given him was, as he had seen at once, perfect for its intended purpose. In it she looked not much more than twenty, young, trusting, and a little helpless. The photographer, using his lights badly, had obliterated any sure indication of her quick intelligence, leaving nothing more than a pretty girl with innocent eyes who, though unmistakably Julie, was yet not Julie at all. A girl who, having already publicly stated that she had seen a facsimile of the devil, might well be considered capable of almost any further imbecility.

The four sketches, alike in the over-all impression they created, yet cunningly dissimilar in detail, made, for general consumption, a pleasantly spine-tingling foil for the photograph which they flanked.

While giving Julie full credit for a picture lay-out which could not have been improved upon, it was the text which went with this, and which he had written *in toto*, which pleased him the most.

To tamper with the truth in so far as he dared was a daily exercise with him, and one to which he was accustomed to give his not inconsiderable wit and energy. This assignment, expressly designed to contain no truth at all, had given him a freedom of action unique in his experience, and he had gone to work on it with unholy pleasure. That he might, in the doing of it, wipe out a six months' old failure, gave an added impetus to his interest in the job.

On the inside pages of the paper he had arranged for a detailed re-hash of the Hurst affair, together with pictures of Deborah, her mother, and a place which he had labelled 'The Abominable Scene of Two Abominable Crimes'. The reward for information leading to the apprehension of the attacker had been revived, and a prominent position given to a boxed editorial demanding that every tree in the ravine be cut into kindling 'to make a funeral pyre for a devil for whom no more fitting inferno can be devised'.

Hot stuff, in every way, Denning thought. Corny, but still hot stuff. I'll hear the woodman's axe in that hole yet.

Briefly he had a vision of the ravine as it would then be, a gentle park and playground, cupped by steep grassy slopes, with no more than a very few shade trees. A natural amphitheatre so exposed to the public gaze that one would hesitate to blow one's nose there. In winter a bowl of virgin white against which the tiny descent of a sparrow would be unlikely to go unremarked: whose snowy sides would be criss-crossed with toboggan tracks, made by children themselves like so many chirping sparrows. Equipped with artificial drainage, and light standards as unobstructed as the moon and stars above, its roads would be a convenience in constant use not only by cars, but by pedestrians as safe, or safer than they would be in their own back gardens.

A happy conception, and one to which he had long ago committed himself and the *Courier*. But, once it was done, with no further possible news value.

Frowning at a front page as sensational as even he could desire, he thought, it will be a Pyrrhic victory, if you win it, Denning my boy. No more rape and sudden death under cover of bosky leafage which could not have been better designed for the purpose by the devil himself. Look thy last on all things unlovely, my boy.

If Tom Denning had been asked whether or not he liked Julie, he would have replied without hesitation that he did. And he would have seen no contradiction in his present willingness to aid and abet her in a scheme which might quite easily result in her death. After all, as he had pointed out to Velyan, it had not been his idea. Business was business, too, and not to be confused with unsolicited missionary work.

He had been strongly tempted to alert his staff to the possibility of getting out an extra in the morning. Reluctant good sense warned him that to do this would be to weaken the tight structure of a trap which, if it were to have any chance of success, must be accepted at face value by everyone but the three who were implicated in it,— Julie, Velyan, and himself. The best he could do would be to spend the night at the police station in the hope that if anything did occur, either a capture metaphorically red-handed, or the regrettable loss of one blonde decoy, he could still move fast enough either to beat the *Sentinel* to the punch, or, at worst, spike an exclusive by simultaneous publication.

You've done the *Sentinel* in the eye this afternoon, anyway, Denning. And if you have to stay up all night to do it again, who are you, my boy, to put creature comfort before the demands of semi-literate vampires who might otherwise be unrefreshed by a goblet of gore with their breakfast cereal?

His glance roving to and fro across the substance of a hypothetical interview which, unsurprisingly, had gone very well from the *Courier*'s point of view, he decided that it would be just as well if he kept out of Greg Markham's way for a time. Although he had no direct evidence to support it, he had a feeling that Greg was both temperamentally and physically capable of giving a poor, but honest newspaperman a quite undeserved beating up.

Without allowing this possibility to disturb him unduly, he nevertheless decided that, all things considered, the police station would not be such a bad place in which to spend the night after all. There were ways and ways of getting news. Bodily harm to the 'special correspondent' who had 'interviewed' Miss Julie Warner was an excess of zeal which he did not feel called upon to display.

Miss Warner herself—if, he thought in parenthesis, she survived to do so—would plead his case. But given a choice between hiding behind a woman's skirt or a police-man's trousers, it seemed to him that the latter offered more cover.

Resuming the toneless whistle which had ceased while he considered the surgeon's probable wrath, he concentrated his attention on what was to him a much pleasanter prospect.

'Miss Warner, while prettily confessing that she did

not always think before she acted, nevertheless had ample evidence in her studio to prove that she was an artist of exceptional merit. Privileged to examine some of her paintings, we were astonished by the perfection of detail in them, recognizing instantly local views familiar to us. Upon being asked whether she had done any of this work from memory, we were further astonished to find that she had. "Would you say that you had a photographic memory?" we asked her. "I don't know," she replied. "Perhaps I have. I've never really thought about it. It's just one of those things, if you know what I mean. I mean to say that I suppose I look at a thing, or a person, and really see it." Cautiously approaching the object of our visit, we asked Miss Warner if she did not think that she could give a better description of the ravine devil in black and white than she had been able to give when questioned verbally. Obviously surprised by this novel idea, she considered it carefully, and then said, with one of her lovely smiles, that she thought she probably could. "I don't know why I didn't think of it myself," she said. "I mean in a way it's so obvious, isn't it? I guess I just haven't been quite myself since that terrible night. I mean I'm so crazy about children, that I'm still dreadfully upset. I can't even see a child fall down at play without running to it. It's a sort of compulsion, I guess you'd say" When we commented on her bravery during the terrible night to which she had referred, she said very simply that she didn't call it bravery, because she just hadn't thought at all. She had simply acted. When asked, with some apology on our part, if she might not try to draw a portrait of the murderer for the *Courier*, she replied without hesitation that she would do anything she humanly could to help in apprehending a monster who must not be allowed to strike again. But this was, she said, something which she would have to work at alone, and that we must give her some time. Upon being asked if she thought she could have it done by the next day, she said that she expected she could do that. It is the *Courier*'s own belief, from what it has seen of Miss Warner's ability, that this may well be the critical nail in the fashioning of a coffin long overdue.'

There was more in the same vein, but, in true journalistic tradition, this added up to no more than a repetition of points already made.

Fatuous to a degree, Denning concluded with satisfaction, and delightfully free of any taint of police spoor. Will you come into my parlour? said the angel to the devil. If he doesn't take a crack at her on the strength of this he'll have my nomination for murderer of the year.

Standing up, taking a last survey of his handiwork, he murmured, 'Good luck, angel. You're going to need it.'

XIV

In the empty silence of an apartment whose quiet was oppressive rather than soothing, Julie mechanically went through the routine of putting away bread and meat and vegetables, the makings of a solitary dinner which she might or might not be there to cook when the time came. Which she might or might not be able to eat, if she did prepare it.

I'm badly frightened, she thought. Only by acknowledging this to myself now, by facing it, can I control it through—how many hours? The balance of the afternoon: three hours. Afternoon and evening: seven hours. The night: an eternity. I'll make what preparations I can, and then I'll find something to do, anything at all, as long as it keeps me from just—waiting.

Long summers in the Maine woods, during which she had been accustomed to going barefoot, had given Julie a lifelong dislike of shoes. She put away the high-heeled pumps out of which she had stepped as soon as the door was locked behind her. In their stead, she selected a pair of flat ballerina shoes with composition rubber soles, and placed them neatly beside a chair near the door. Across the chair she laid a loose, dark coat, in the pocket of which she tucked a thick scarf, trying not to allow her conscious mind to dwell on her reason for wanting a scarf at all. That she had no intention of using it for her head was at once apparent, for, pinning her hair up, she tied a triangle of black silk around it. Then she changed from the grey suit into a long-sleeved black sweater, dark slacks, and a pair of black wool socks. With her slender height, it was a becoming outfit, and one which she often wore when working both indoors and out. That it should suit her had nothing to do with her present choice.

She crossed to the desk, opened the top drawer, and from amongst a miscellany of drawing utensils took the small spring-knife which she used for sharpening pencils. Before slipping it into the right-hand pocket of her slacks, she pressed the button which released the blade, and looked for an instant at tempered steel which, though it would probably prove entirely futile, nevertheless gave her some courage. Even a single claw was better than no claws at all.

You are not Deborah, or Susie, she told herself hardily. You are not a child, and you will not be taken unaware. Pull yourself together, Julie. You have real physical strength, and you can fight as they could not. But will he come after you, bare-handed, as he did with them? Will he stick to his pattern, or will he change it with you? And if he does, in what way? Stop it, Julie, stop it!

Through the west window she could see the treetops of the ravine writhing and twisting in ugly defiance of a wind which reached down to pluck at them from a fast-moving cloud wrack.

Greg, she cried silently, Greg, I need you! And so strong was her desire for even a glimpse of him, that she no longer made any pretence to herself about her feelings for him. Desperately she searched her mind for some way in which to establish a contact with him other than the actual one denied her by her own actions. I'll tell them at home about him, she thought. That should help. Written words are a poor medium in which to describe such a man, but even if I can't do him justice, I can perhaps draw them all a little closer to me now in a letter about him, and to them.

Refusing to look at a telephone which, though silent, seemed to shiver and vibrate on the verge of screaming at her, she sat down at the desk. But with a piece of empty notepaper in front of her, it was not easy to begin. All the things she must not say were so interwoven with what she could say that to disentangle them needed more of her mind than she could detach from minutes which, though they dragged more slowly than any others in her life, still moved inexorably towards darkness. Darkness, literal and metaphorical, which already seemed to throw its shadow across her. For it would not come until after dark, of that she was morally certain. And as yet it was no more than three o'clock. Still one hour until the *Courier* would be on the streets. Two hours until the November darkness would begin to close in.

Make a start, Julie. A start of some kind. Begin as you would have begun if none of this had happened.

'Darlings,
      This has been a lovely week. Have been painting like mad, and think you'll like what I've done. Expect to have about twenty canvases to bring home with me at Christmas. The autumn colours still linger. Even now there are traces of bronze, and gold, and red... red... red....'

Blindly she looked at a pen which had snapped in two between her fingers. Then, slowly crumpling the sheet of paper, she got up and went to the window in search of the only contact with the outside world which could have any present reality for her. Shielded by the curtain, she watched the people passing on the street below her, and tried to identify the detective who must be somewhere not far from the mouth of the alley which led to her door. But although she watched both the street, and alternately, from the north window, the parking lot behind the garage, she could not place him. There was nobody who reappeared more often than was consistent with shopping in the area, or who seemed in any way out of step with a shifting scene singular only in that it was so very ordinary. From time to time she allowed her attention to wander to the antics of a small white dog being exercised by a nondescript man on the edge of the ravine, but never for long enough that she might miss someone passing on the street.

Her first intimation that dusk was already gathering was when the globe of the light standard directly across the street glowed with sudden light. A radiance too feeble to penetrate the wall of blackness behind it where, in the ravine, night had already staked its claim.

So soon, Julie thought in quick panic. Looking at her watch, she saw that it was too soon. Saw that the loose garland of lights surrounding the ravine had, for what they were worth, been turned on some forty minutes ahead of their usual time. Torn between despair that it should still be no later than twenty minutes past four, and gratitude for this proof that in all possible ways she was being protected, she turned abruptly back to the room, seeking something with which to occupy her hands, if not her mind.

In a half-light where familiar pieces of furniture loomed unfamiliar, and security as she had always known it had ceased to exist, her eyes searched in vain for a task, no matter how trivial, which might ease the minutes through their slow march towards oblivion.

The soft, rasping scratch on her door shocked her as much as if the nails responsible had scraped across a raw nerve-end. Her face drained of colour, stifling the sound she had almost made, she stood motionless, a prey to two violently conflicting emotions. Fear for, and something very like fear of the partially destroyed girl who now crouched against her door on a landing which must be in almost total darkness.

The scratching recommenced, abrading the silence with terrible unemphatic persistence.

How long will she stay there? Julie thought wildly. If I move, if I make the slightest sound, she will know I am here, will go on making that hideous noise until I either let her in or go mad. Of all the people I have ever known, she is the one I least want to see now, the one who should be furthest from this place at this moment. Deborah, for God's sake, go away, go away!

For perhaps as much as five minutes the scratching continued, while Julie slid closer and closer towards the edge of her endurance. With too vivid an imagination, she could see the lower door opening without a sound; could see a shape, darker than the one already on the landing, creep upwards to strike where it had struck once before; could hear, as if it were already in her ears, the throttled cry of a creature caught in a narrow trap from which there was no escape except through the door she had promised not to open.

I can't stand it, Julie thought. No matter what I promised, I cannot stand this. I will have to let her in, and when I do it will be the end of my own fine gesture. I can not look into those vacant eyes, and have any courage left.

With as little warning as when it had begun, the scratching stopped. But Julie, her ears straining, heard what she had not heard earlier, the soft shuffle of movement on the stair treads. Following the furtive retreat downwards, step by step, with the whole of her attention, she was finally aware of the faint vibration of a door being opened and closed.

Trembling with reaction, she tiptoed swiftly to the kitchen window, and was just in time to see a thin, hunched figure scurry away amongst the cars behind a garage now closed for the night.

With unsteady fingers she took a packet of cigarettes from the shelf above the sink, lit one, and, momentarily dazzled by the match flame, leaned against the sink before going back into the studio to draw the curtains. At the north window she did not pause. When she came to the view of the street, and the ravine, restless blue eyes searched again for a man whose features it would have been a comfort to know. But there was no-one other than a stout woman carrying a paper bag, and a young man and a girl with their arms laced around one another. Even the little white dog and his indulgent owner had gone home.

She was on the point of pulling the curtains across, when, the motion arrested, she concentrated on a tall figure which had just come into her range of vision. But it turned out to be simply another man with a dog; this time a big Alsatian on a lead.

Making certain that there were no cracks between the curtains, Julie switched on every light in the studio, a slender figure who had discovered a definite, if temporary purpose. She then worked back through the stack of canvases against the wall until she reached her objective in the cruelly faithful travesty of a human being still called— because no matter what else changes a label remains the same—Deborah.

A portrait, painted on good canvas with good quality oil paints, is a difficult thing to blot out of all existence. To paint over it, is to conceal it, and no more. It is still there, can still be restored by anyone with sufficient knowledge and patience to do so. To tear it up is impossible. To cut it up is to reduce it to a jigsaw of dismembered fragments which, even in mutilation, preserve all the component parts of the original. Only in a very hot fire can it be completely annihilated.

Having no fireplace, Julie, bent on immediate destruction, set the portrait up on the easel, and did the best she could under the circumstances.

With her spring-knife, she slashed the canvas to ribbons, wishing in her bitter sorrow for the girl herself that what she did could represent something other than the destruction of a soul already dead. Memory repeated Greg's question of the previous night, and her own negative to the effect that she could not have done this portrait in reverse. And she wondered if what she did now with such determined fury might not be a reversal of the old superstition that one could kill by sticking pins into a waxen image. If she might not, in obliterating a Deborah without a soul, be returning that soul to her.

Breathing unevenly, she stepped back from a tattered ruin, and told herself, you are too fanciful, Julie. But not so fanciful that you imagined a devil where no devil was. Go and eat, Julie. The night still lies ahead of you. And even the self-condemned should eat.

She passed the telephone on her way to the kitchen, and thought, out of that square black bottle the evil genius of the ravine will materialize if he is to materialize at all. And suddenly none of it made any sense. Least of all the part she had elected to play. Nina was dead, and had been dead for five long years. Susie was dead. Those were stark, undeniable facts. Everything else seemed hazy and unreal, as unreal as the long afternoon behind her which, without tangible threat, had quietly merged with early evening. Struck by the quietness, she realized that the wind had died, leaving isolated street sounds blurred by no more than their individual distance from her.

As she laid a single place at the kitchen table, and put butter into a frying pan, the idea that a police detective even now lay hidden on the floor of the station-wagon would have been ridiculous if it had not been for her own reflection in the mirror over the table. Her face, strained and pale, framed in the black silk turban, was mute evidence that there was nothing even remotely ridiculous in the situation in which she had placed herself.

She had not expected that she would be able to eat the food she had prepared. To her surprise, she was ravenously hungry. The green and white electric clock on the wall said eleven minutes past six when she started her dinner. It said twenty-seven minutes past six when she finished.

At twenty-nine minutes past six the telephone rang.

This is it, Julie told herself with frozen calm. It could be Greg. It could be Clare. It could be any one of half a dozen people. But it isn't. How did Captain Velyan phrase it? I am to agree with whatever suggestion is made, 'no matter how ordinary or far-fetched'. I will do this part better sitting down.

She came to rest on the edge of a chair beside the telephone table, and took out the cork which was to release an evil genius. 'Hello?'

'Hello—Miss Warner?' The man's voice was thick with some apparently ungovernable emotion.

'Yes. Speaking.'

'John Grey here. Is Barbara with you?'

For a fraction of a second Julie was thrown off balance, wondered if her every instinct could be wrong. Her doubt put a naturalness into her voice that she might not otherwise have achieved. 'No! Did you think she was?'

His words charged with anxiety, the man replied, 'We don't know what to think. We're out of our minds with worry. Barbara has been in bed all day. Flu, and a high temperature. We went down to dinner, my wife and I. My wife ran upstairs a few minutes later for a handkerchief, and looked in on Barbara. And, my God, Miss Warner, she isn't there!'

No, I wasn't wrong, and I know already what is coming next. 'Have you searched the house, Mr. Grey?'

'Yes. Of course. She's not here, and her coat is gone. Nothing else. Just her coat.'

It was not difficult for Julie to sound tense in her turn.

She was taut as a bow-string. 'What made you think she might have come to me, in her nightclothes—on the other side of town?'

'She has been talking about you all day, Miss Warner. About you—and Susan.'

That was a mistake. If it were really John Grey, he would have said Susie, not Susan. 'What do you think has happened? Where do you think she can have got to?'

No father could have sounded more distraught. And no voice could have been more effectively disguised than by that seeming distress.

'This will probably sound mad to you, Miss Warner. But we—her mother and I—are convinced that she, oh, my God—that she had gone down into the ravine. She has been almost delirious all afternoon. She seemed to think that there was something she could do for Susan. Seemed to have forgotten that poor little Susan was dead. Seemed to have the idea that Susan was in the ravine, and that she must help her.'

You can't act, Julie, but you've got to, now. It's your cue, your initiative. You are Red Riding-Hood and as credulous as they come. 'Oh, Mr. Grey, that's terrible! I must help, somehow. Tell me what I can do to help you?'

'I don't think, if she isn't with you, that there is anything——'

Very crafty. Still your initiative, Julie. 'There must be something! Barby, perhaps alone down in—no, I can't bear it! Please, tell me what I can do? Have you called the police?'

'No. I called you first. I thought—look, Miss Warner. You can help, if you will. No more time must be lost. Too much has been lost already. Can you start down from your side of the ravine? I'll get my car out at once, and come down from our side. My wife will call the police. They will be there almost as soon as we will. We can cover the bottom of the ravine from three angles in that way. I know it's an awful thing to ask——' the muffled, agonized voice broke, and then went on, 'it's too much. But nevertheless I ask it. For Barbara.'

'Nothing would be too much for Barbara,' Julie replied with complete sincerity. Barbara is not in the ravine, but I am doing this for her just the same. 'I will start at once.'

'I don't know how to thank you, Miss Warner. I'll be there ahead of you if I can.'

Will you come into my parlour? With no pleasure at all, I will. 'I'm leaving now, Mr. Grey.'

As she listened to the singing silence of an abruptly severed connection, Julie bit her lip until it hurt. Far-fetched? In some ways, very. In any way that counted, not at all. For if it had, in truth, been Barbara's father, she would have done exactly what she was about to do. Tom Denning, in the *Courier*, must have depicted her as either very foolish, or very fond of children, or both. Probably both. For Denning was clever, as clever as they came, and he wanted her in that ravine, alive or dead. It would not, she knew, make too much difference to him which.

Leaving the lights blazing behind her, she stepped into her shoes as she put on her coat. Car keys? Yes. Knife? Yes. Scarf? Yes.

At the lower door she hesitated briefly before turning to her right and running down the alley and across the dark parking space to the station-wagon. She wrenched open the door beside the driver's seat, slid in, and slammed the door after her. It could have happened between the apartment and the car. It hadn't. It was to be the ravine.

'Detective Wingham here. Don't turn your head, Miss Warner.'

'I won't.'

'Take your time getting out on to the street. Our contact car will pass in front of your building again in a minute and a half. Give them a chance to pick us up.'

Julie fitted her key into the ignition with a steady hand. 'They can make a report, but they won't be able to follow us where we're going without giving the whole thing away. We're on our way into the ravine, Mr. Wingham.'

The cool, decisive voice behind her appeared undisturbed. 'Captain Velyan recognized that possibility. Can you hand a glove or a scarf back to me?'

Puzzled, Julie pulled out her scarf, and dropped it over the back of the seat as she swung the big stationwagon out on to Ravine Street. A small panel truck passed in front of her, and then as she straightened the wheel she saw the headlights of a car a block ahead flicker once.

'Those are our people, Miss Warner. You can go ahead now as fast as you like.' His tone changing, becoming at once softer and more authoritative, Julie heard him say, and obviously not to her, 'Friend, Baron, friend.'

'You're not alone?' she asked, startled.

He sounded amused. 'No. And you are about to be investigated by the party of the third part. One Alsatian. Try not to jerk away from him. It's important that he gets you placed properly. Friend—Baron. Friend.'

Something cold and damp touched Julie's cheek, and in the rearview mirror she could see the dog's big head beside her own before he dropped down out of sight again.

The dog had neither growled, nor made a stir of any kind when she had jumped so precipitately into the car. 'He's well trained, your dog,' she commented.

'He wouldn't be much good if he weren't,' the man replied calmly. 'He answers to hand commands as well as spoken ones. Before you got into the car he had been told not to move. He wouldn't have so much as twitched if you had walked over him. On the other hand—a signal from me, which you would not have heard, and he would have killed you.'

Slowing down as she came to the spot where the road, which she must follow once again, plunged into the ravine, Julie said thoughtfully, 'I saw you on the street just at dusk. Earlier there was a man with a little white dog. I didn't think——'

'Neither you nor anyone else was supposed to think anything. A baby carriage is something else that people don't think about. Dogs and babies, they're so obvious nobody really sees them.'

He's talking to steady me. And he's succeeding. How perceptive of Captain Velyan to have chosen a man like this. A tough cop would have given me no feeling of security at all. This road is even worse than it was three nights ago. Only three nights? For me, it is several centuries. I don't feel frightened yet. I don't feel anything. What a god-awful place this is. And how quiet.

She took the dark descent slowly, her grip on the wheel sure and firm. Nevertheless the tyres slid at each turn, first the right fender and then the left almost brushing against the ebony solidity of tunnel walls which seemed to press in against a slippery track they would crush out of existence if they could.

'Miss Warner.'

'Yes?'

'What was the story you were given?'

'Barbara Grey. Susie Philips' friend. She is supposed to be delirious with flu, to have left the house to look for Susie whom she no longer believes to be dead. The man who telephoned said he was her father. He is to meet me here in search of her. I was told that the police would be coming from the south end of the ravine.'

'He took your reaction at face value?'

'I swear to it.'

There was a brief silence, and then Wingham said, 'He'll come down on foot. Almost certainly from the west side near the hospital. By following one of the foot-paths he can get down faster than we can. He will be there ahead of us. Probably somewhere on the flat stretch of road at the bottom. How is your nerve, Miss Warner?'

'All right, I think.'

'Then this is what I want you to do. When we get down on to the level, can you make a convincing show of getting stuck, of being unable to go any further in the car? Either forwards or backwards.'

'It will be convincing,' Julie told him grimly, 'chiefly because I think it will be true.'

'All right. Once you're stuck, stall your motor, and run it off the battery. Your battery was changed this afternoon for one with so little juice in it that your headlights will go dim almost at once. After a minute or so, flicker your headlights a few times, and then turn them out. Got the idea?'

'Yes.'

'Good. As effective a pretence of complete battery failure as you can manage. While you're doing this will you roll down the two front windows as far as they'll go? They'll run smoothly. All the windows and doors of your car have been oiled.'

'By a man with a baby, I presume?' Julie said, easing carefully over a thick branch, fallen across the road, which sank without cracking into the heavy mud.

The detective chuckled. 'More or less. Now there'll be one critical moment after the lights go out which we have to make full use of. Listen carefully, and do exactly what I say when the moment comes. Slide across into the right-hand seat, lean out of the window, and call "Mr. Grey". Call twice, and if you sound scared, so much the better. While you're doing this, the dog and I are going out through the door on the driver's side and into the trees beyond the edge of the road. I have a gun and a flashlight. The instant we're out, get to the back of the car. Lie down on the floor. Keep still. And stay there.'

One more sharp twist in the road, and they would be on the bottom of the ravine.

'You think he'll come to the car, even if he doesn't hear me again?'

'I'm almost certain he will.'

'And if he doesn't?'

'End of this particular line,' Wingham told her curtly. 'Captain Velyan's orders are that you are to be exposed to no more risk than is implicit in your being here at all. I will be covering the door on the driver's side, and from a distance of not more than fifteen feet. If and when he comes, and can't find you, he will have to show a light, if he has not done so before. I take over at that point, and Baron, if I need him. Can I count on you to stay where I've told you to stay, so that I can shoot if I have to?'

Weak with relief that she would not have to leave the car as she had braced herself to do if necessary, Julie nodded. 'I'll stay there.'

'Right. We won't talk from here on in.'

Side-slipping, exactly as it had done when she last came this way, the station-wagon slid down into the close-grown confines of a gully where pale streamers of mist hung motionless against a sable backdrop of wet, impenetrable silence. Here the ravine became a presence in itself, heavy with the corruption of its own rotting vegetation, mired in its own rank slime, polluted by its own odours.

Oppressed equally by memory, and an atmosphere redolent with unseen menace, Julie tried to close her mind to everything but the instructions she had been given. But, try as she would, she could not rid herself of the feeling that just ahead of twin beams of light, diffused by the mist, a small figure in a red raincape was running, running, running—too fast for her to catch up with it, but still not fast enough.

Braking against the accelerator, she allowed the wheels to spin too hard, to dig themselves deep into wet clay. With a detached portion of her brain, she accepted the fact that she had done this part of her job so well that it would take a tow-truck to move the station-wagon from where it was. On either side of the road tangled thickets promised cover for hunters and hunted alike. It worked both ways.

Stalling the motor as she had been told to do, hearing it cough, she pressed her foot hard on the starter while with either hand she wound down windows which responded with soundless ease. The motor itself turned off, she saw that the headlights were dimming already. Not too fast, Julie. Give it a minute—and another. Now. From now on there will be nothing but darkness. As she thought this, she shifted her hand to the light-switch, turned it slowly off and on three times, and finally off. Then she slid over onto the seat to her right in a darkness which appalled her with the completeness of its obliteration of all things visible.

'Mr. Grey!'

Touched with genuine hysteria, scarcely recognizable as her own, the voice was a voice crying in the wilderness.

'Mr. Grey!'

By the time the second call had faded from the cold, damp air, Wingham and the big dog, moving with incredible speed and quiet, had climbed past her and gone, the only proof of their passing a lingering musky scent from the Alsatian.

Blindly, in every way, Julie followed the pattern which had been laid down for her. Struggling with unreasonable panic, she eased herself into the most comfortable position possible on the floor behind the back seats. Not until she had done this, did she realize that she was facing the rear doors rather than the front of the station-wagon as she would have chosen had she stopped to think independently. If I move gently, I can turn over, she told herself. But the quality of the silence wrapping itself, second by second, more tightly about her, bound her as she was.

Listening to that silence, feeling her muscles gradually

contracting until she was rigid from head to toe, a tiny sucking noise below her as the station-wagon settled more deeply in the mud was like an explosion in its effect on her overstrained nerves.

And when the doors close against her face swung open without fore-warning of any kind, as noiseless as the night itself, it was to find her mentally clear, but physically paralyzed, incapable of the slightest sound or movement.

In a void no less black than it had been, almost touching her, was a presence which, sensing her nearness as clearly as she sensed it, now rested as motionless as she herself. If it had been carefully explained to her, Julie could not have known more precisely what had happened and what was about to happen. Guided by the sound of her voice when she called he had come not to the driver's side of the car but to the offside. Reaching silently through the open window, finding her gone, he had circled to the back, intending to climb in and ambush her inside the car itself.

The dog would know all this. But the dog would not move until told to move.

Her vocal chords as useless as her limbs, she knew that she was nevertheless communicating her frozen terror to the invisible executioner standing over her, as clearly as though she had shrieked it aloud. Eyes wide and staring in darkness which pressed against them with a weight of its own, she gave away the knowledge that she was a sacrifice tethered to a stake from which she could not break free.

Drowning in a bottomless well of terror, deeper by far than the ravine which had shackled her with its own impalpable aura of evil, she felt hands exploring her body, feeling their way cautiously upward, and, inhuman in texture and intent, gently closing around her throat.

XV

At five-thirty that afternoon a copy of the *Courier* was laid on Mrs. Wylie's desk. At five-thirty-one she was trying to contact Gregory Markham on the surgical floor.

'Third floor? Mrs. Wylie speaking. Can you get Dr. Markham for me? It's very urgent.'

'I'm sorry, Mrs. Wylie, but he's operating. Dr. Abrams is free. Shall I put him through to you?'

'No, thank you. Only Dr. Markham will do. Have you any idea when he will be free?'

'It's an abdominal, Mrs. Wylie, so I just can't say.'

That could mean one hour—two hours. It could mean anything. 'Thank you, Miss Best,' she said evenly.

She put down the telephone, and stared again at the glaring implications of the *Courier*'s front page. How long until the one man who must not see it, inevitably did? Or had he seen it already? She turned her head and looked up at a call-board which showed arrows beside half the names listed, but not beside the only one which counted. I can't just sit here, and do nothing, she thought frantically. Dear God, I must do something, and do it now.

She got up abruptly, the paper under her arm, and walked across the lobby to the switch-board. 'Jennie, I'm feeling sick. I'm going home. Will you take over the desk for me?'

'Okay, Mrs. Wylie,' the girl said. 'Just a minute while I speak to Mabel here. You sure aren't looking so good.'

Managing not to run, Mrs. Wylie signalled to the elevator man to wait for her. When she reached the third floor, she turned down the corridor towards Greg's office. In the office, she put the *Courier* in the top drawer of the desk. On a piece of Greg's stationery she scribbled a hasty note, put it in an envelope, and, marking it urgent, left it under a desk lamp which she turned on before leaving. Perhaps the police would listen to what she had to say, and perhaps they wouldn't. But she knew that she would never be able to forgive herself if she did not do everything in her power to make them take some action at once. Seeing in her mind a slim, black-clad figure which, even in daylight, moved with the softness of a hunting leopard, she really did feel ill.

It was not until six-thirty that Greg, aching with fatigue, walked into his office to notice, with quick irritation, that somebody had been in and left the light on.

Two minutes later, his grey eyes terrifying in their hard fury, he slammed down the receiver of his telephone on a continuing busy signal. If Julie's line was busy, it meant she was still there, and still nominally safe. Fifteen, perhaps twenty minutes by car. But on foot, across the ravine— ten minutes. He wrenched open a drawer in which he had recently put a revolver and a powerful flashlight. He slipped the automatic into his pocket, checked the flashlight and, thanking God that all hospital personnel wore rubber-soled shoes, raced out of the room and flung himself at the stairs, going down them three at a time. And as he went, he promised himself that if he could get to her in time, she would not go free until a devil with flaring nostrils and the flat lips of a medieval torturer had been put where he could never again sate his lust for killing and for little girls. If necessary, Greg thought grimly, he would handcuff Julie to him; eat with her, sleep with her: and be damned to her protests, the conventions, his job, everything on earth but her safety.

Running fast across the car park, skirting people who were no more than obstacles to be avoided, whose stares meant less than nothing at all to him, he passed from the harsh radiance of arc lights into the outer shadows of the ravine's edge.

To cross the ravine at night by a maze of trails, as he intended to do, would have been madness had he not known it almost as well as he knew the hospital corridors. A boyhood spent in the town had given him a knowledge of the ravine equalled by few, and trails once beaten over difficult ground were, he knew, rarely deviated from. Narrow, steeply angled, they were a labyrinth which nevertheless represented the line of least resistance.

Breaking through a wiry thicket of bushes between two moss-covered beech trees, he vaulted into a transverse, pebbled slit which was more water-course than path. Sure-footed, maintaining an instinctive balance, he descended by the most direct and most precipitous route to the ravine floor, guided as much by memory as by the strong white shaft of his flashlight. To lose his way even briefly was to lose seconds every one of which he considered precious beyond measure, and he concentrated on avoiding this to the exclusion of all else, ignoring branches which tore at his clothes and twice raked his face. He gained the level at the bottom, and struck across flat ground with the same determined singleness of purpose, paying as little attention to sludge in places inches deep, as he did to heavy undergrowth.

If he had had to depend entirely on his flashlight for guidance, he would have kept it trained close to the earth; and, as he approached the road, might have crossed it without picking up the fleeting gleam of chrome which betrayed the station-wagon, unlit, apparently deserted, some fifty feet away on his right.

He swerved so suddenly he almost slipped and fell on the greasy surface of the road. But the automatic was in his right hand even as he shouted her name. 'Julie! Julie—for the love of God, answer me!'

Of all the answers he might have received, the one he got was probably the most unexpected. Still more than twenty feet from her car, he was intercepted by a man who demanded curtly, 'Who are you? And what are you doing here?'

Recognizing the detective against the light of a torch less powerful than his own, Greg said savagely, 'So the police are in this, too, are they? Where is Miss Warner?'

Wingham, coming closer, the Alsatian a bristling shadow at his side, said, 'Oh, it's you, Doctor. Down, Baron. Heel!'

'Where is Miss Warner?'

'Dr. Markham,' Wingham said stiffly, 'Captain Velyan instructed me that you——'

Greg pocketed his gun, and his voice was dangerously quiet. 'If you don't answer my question, and answer it now, both you and that bloody dog of yours will suffer for it.'

With a small shrug, the detective gave him his answer, but not without sarcasm. 'You might have chosen a more suitable occasion for heroics, Doctor. Miss Warner is in the back of her car, quite safe, and if you had not——'

For the second time, Greg gave him no time to finish. Brushing past him, he strode towards the station-wagon, his frown deepening as he saw the rear doors standing wide open.

'Julie!'

As long as he lived, he was never to forget her face as he saw it then; blue eyes fixed and staring, scarcely sane; lipstick, a doll's mouth painted against stiff pallor from which all the life blood seemed to have drained away. And below a pointed, rigid chin two livid marks at the base of a white throat.

He dipped his light so that she could see him clearly, and with a terrible effort of will restrained himself from lifting her into his arms. Training overcoming instinct, he knew that to touch her at all, until she made the first move, was impossible. That she was seeing him was obvious from the contraction and focus of pupils which had been wide and black. But there was as yet no proof that her shocked mind had accepted his identity.

Striving for an easy blend of concern and irritation, knowing that his tone was much more important than the words he used, he chided her gently. 'So this is the way you look after yourself when I'm not there to do it for you. You plot and plan yourself into a position which looks to me, offhand, as if it might have been awkward. For your information, I have decided, as of this minute, that twenty-four hours constitutes an acquaintanceship more than long enough to warrant my running your life for you.'

Aware that Wingham had moved up behind him, he made a quick gesture which commanded him to silence.

'You see,' he continued to Julie, smiling a little, 'I'm a strong-minded individual who has no intention of coming home to find, instead of my favourite dinner— which is steak, by the way—a note to this effect, "Gone to ravine. Back soon. I hope." In fact, whatever you may think to the contrary, you are never'—he paused, and repeated the last word, underlining it intentionally—'*never* coming down here again. If I weren't so annoyed with you, I might do something about that neck of yours. From the look of it, it's going to be damned stiff before morning.'

Seeing her hand twitch, and then begin to move hesitantly towards her throat, he knew relief as shattering as his fear for her had been. But still he did not touch her. If possible she must be made to come all the way back first, back out of a hell he could imagine only too well. Her courage had kept her conscious, but in doing so had exposed her to horror which only she could reduce to a proportion which she could handle.

'If I were you, my darling,' he went on easily, 'I would ask the next doctor you happen to run into, to have a look at that neck. He could probably do something about it. He might even be glad to.'

Gingerly her fingers touched her throat. 'Greg——'

The hoarse whisper was the last assurance he needed. Sweeping her up in his arms, he held her close, unaware either that he had dropped his torch or that it had been picked up for him.

The detective, knowing that he owed this man an apology for which there were no words, whistled softly to the Alsatian he had left some yards behind him. Guiding the dog's nose towards footprints which had already begun to lose their shape in the yellow slime, he whispered, 'Get him, Baron. Go get him!'

A moment later the great beast vanished into the surrounding darkness.

Julie, her whole frame shaken by long, spasmodic sobs, murmured thickly, 'Greg. Get me out of here. Please. Get me out of here now!'

Not only for Julie's sake, but because of the sombre malevolence of the place in which they stood, Wingham spoke very quietly. 'Her car is in up to the axles. I'll have a squad car down in a matter of minutes.'

The shrill blast of his police whistle stirred no echoes in the heavy silence of the ravine, but it accomplished its purpose. Almost immediately, on all three roads—leading from the water tower, the main square, and the hospital— the lights of cars could be seen slowly winding down three separate descents. Grudgingly, Greg conceded that Velyan had been well enough prepared for all reasonable contingencies. Which, however, did not exonerate him from failing to anticipate the unreasonable in a context where reason, as such, obviously played so small a part.

'Greg.'

'Yes, darling?'

'I can't stay here.'

'It won't be more than a few minutes now.'

Pulling away from him, while still clinging to his hand, Julie said in a voice which rose sharply towards the end of her sentence, 'I can't stay here!'

'All right,' Greg told her. 'Then we'll leave. Wingham, can you light the way for us? We're going to start walking.'

Even with Greg's arm to support her, Julie could feel the mud tugging at her feet as if the ravine itself was trying to hold her back, hideously loath to unwind the invisible tentacles it had wrapped around her in a moment when, unhampered, she would not have lost her courage.

And even though she could see that they were close to the car approaching then, she thought frantically, we must go faster—faster! For, irrational as she knew it to be, she was much more afraid of the ravine than of a man who, uninterrupted, would have killed her at the very least. It was the ravine, like some dark primeval force, which she had felt to be her deadliest enemy.

This was a truth which, if it had not already been clear, would have become immediately apparent to her when the police car arrived at the top of the last gradient. For in the prosaic atmosphere of shops and sidewalks, and people on their way to the second show at the neighbourhood movie, she recovered her self-possession to an extent which astonished Wingham who, less perceptive than the surgeon, had expected that she might even now give way to hysterics.

Seated between the two men in the back of the car, she turned and really looked at the detective for the first time. 'Mr. Wingham, I'm afraid I let you down very badly. I——' and then she stopped.

Wingham, who knew why she did not go on, said mildly, 'You didn't expect an old man, Miss Warner?'

Some of the colour returned to Julie's white cheeks. Confused, she said, 'You're not an old man.' But he had been right. She had assumed he was young, just why she could not have said, and to find that he was a grey-haired man in his late fifties both increased her respect for him, and made her own weakness seem worse. Impulsively, she touched his arm. 'I let you down,' she repeated. 'I'm sorry.'

'It was my job to protect you,' Wingham said soberly. 'And I made a bad job of it. Let's leave it at that. Here's your apartment now.' He leaned forward and spoke to the policeman at the wheel. 'On your left, Peters. Third building in the block.' To the second policeman, another official silhouette in the front seat, he said, 'I'll leave you here, Wilson. Patrol this block. We'll be in touch with you.'

Greg's voice, decisive, brooking no argument, calmly countermanded this last order. 'No one is to patrol Miss Warner's apartment, now or later. Enough damage has been done without that. There is just a chance that our man in the ravine still suspects nothing. He never saw you, Wingham. Never knew you were there. If he had, he would not have been there himself, I assure you. All he knows is that I was there. He will probably think that Miss Warner called me before leaving her apartment, and that I, in my turn, called the police. By the time you get back to headquarters, I'll have called Captain Velyan. In the meantime I'll make myself personally responsible for Miss Warner's safety.'

'Since when have I taken my orders from the medical profession?' Wingham asked, but he did so without heat. It was his way of offering the apology he owed, and of admitting that the surgeon made sense.

The car pulled into the kerb, and Greg, his hand on the door, said, smiling, 'Will you accede to my request?'

'Pending Captain Velyan's agreement. Yes.'

'He'll agree.'

The first thing that Julie looked at when she walked

into the brightly lit apartment was the clock which had measured the dragging minutes of an afternoon and early evening which might have belonged to another incarnation, so brutally had they been pushed back in time by more recent terror.

Aware that Greg had gone straight to the telephone and had already made his connection, she crossed to a wall mirror and studied marks on her throat, now turning purple, which were her only tangible evidence that someone had tried to throttle her. Without those bruises, she realized that she would no longer quite believe this. Die—death. Experimentally she said the words over in her mind, but during the preceding three days she had heard them too often for them to mean much in relationship to herself. They were words indissolubly welded to a small, mutilated violin—to a red raincape which had looked like a spreading pool of blood. The quick and the dead. Impossible to place herself in the latter category. It was not the threat of death, she thought slowly, which frightened me so terribly in the ravine, but something much, much worse. The spirit of all evil was in that place when Susie died, and it was there again tonight.

'Hurt?'

She raised her eyes until they met and were held by those of the man now reflected behind her. 'A little. But not nearly so much as my pride.'

In a way I should be grateful for her particular brand of stubborn courage, Greg reflected, because I'm going to need it tomorrow. It's my assurance that here, in this place which is hers and familiar to her, she will be able to do what I want her to do. 'Too much pride and too little sense,' he told her gently.

'How did you know to come there, Greg?'

'I didn't. I saw the *Courier*, and took the shortest route to the apartment of a damned little fool determined to martyr herself.'

'I had no intention of being a martyr. I may be a fool, but I'm not martyr material. You know that.'

He laid his hands on her shoulders, and turned her to face him. 'Yes, I know that. But you nearly were one. Julie, are you going to stop fighting me?'

'Greg—I can't stop! Even now, I must go on with it, if there is any way in which I can. I must go on until Barbara, until all the Barbaras in this town are safe again. I'm a horrible coward, but there are things I'm more afraid of than this.' Her fingers brushed her throat.

'You're no coward, Julie. But dead, as you will be if you don't let me take over, you will be no good to yourself or to the Barbaras.'

Searching his face, learning nothing from it that she did not already know, she said hesitantly, 'Take over? But what can you do?'

'Given any luck at all, I can get him,' he told her with such quiet savagery she was almost frightened of him.

'Then you actually *do* know who he is?'

'Yes.'

'And you'll tell me now?'

'After you've had a drink, and something to eat. I called you at noon today. I was ready to tell you then, but you weren't here.'

Why should I feel so guilty, Julie wondered. And realized that it was because to herself, if not to him, she had already granted his right to know what she was doing, and why. 'I was at—at the police station.'

'Tell me, Julie, who was originally responsible for this evening's Grand Guignol? You, or Denning, or Velyan?'

'I was.'

'I guessed as much. And you had no trouble with Denning, but needed to apply pressure tactics to enlist Velyan. Am I right?'

Julie had seen his face darken as he mentioned Tom Denning. 'It was entirely my idea,' she said. 'You mustn't blame Mr. Denning.'

167

'If he's wise, he'll keep out of my way for some time to come,' Greg told her shortly. 'He did his part altogether too well. I wonder if it had quite got through to you, Julie, that your precious scheme is still as much in force as when you launched it. You expected to produce either nothing at all, or a decisive finish of some kind or other. Well, you produced something which was decisive only in that it established beyond question that the killer now considers you a genuine threat to him. It's either you or him. Have you taken that in, with all that it implies?'

Julie gave him complete honesty. 'In a way I have. In a way I suppose I haven't. My part in it doesn't seem quite real. Everything else is almost too real. But not what I myself am doing.'

'Your trouble is that you think too much about other people, Julie. You need someone who will put you first. Do I do that with your permission, or without it?'

'I—Greg—please——'

'Take that damn black thing off your head,' he said softly. 'I like to see your hair.'

This is not the time, Julie thought, to let him guess that just looking at him leaves me weak. But she unwound the black scarf from around her head. 'You know now where to find the makings of a drink,' she told him impersonally. 'Will you look after that while I find something we can eat?'

He followed her through to the kitchen. 'Sandwiches, or something equally simple, will you, Julie? I've asked Captain Velyan to come here at ten, and we need time in which to talk first.'

'Coffee?'

'Thank you. What was the lure, Julie? What took you into the ravine?'

Concisely, Julie told him, and he silently damned Tom Denning for the wickedly clever way in which he had mapped out just such a possibility. While telling the innocent nothing, he had issued, in print, not just a general invitation to the guilty, but a specific one with all the latent news value possible, no matter which way the dice fell. Tom Denning liked jam on his corpses.

'You haven't actually seen today's *Courier*, have you?' he asked.

'No. Should I?'

Not altogether truthfully, he said, 'You know pretty well how it was laid out, I imagine. How will you have your drink? Same prescription as last time?'

'Yes, please. Very easy on the whisky.'

Without consulting him, Julie laid places at the kitchen table rather than on the gateleg table in the studio. But if she had thought to reduce their physical awareness of one another by remaining in the kitchen, she knew as soon as they say down that she had failed to do so. If anything, it heightened a feeling of intimacy usually found only at breakfast after a much greater intimacy. The thoughts of one paralleling the thoughts of the other, they ate in silence and with more haste than was necessary. But when, with mutual relief, they returned to the studio, they had acknowledged without the necessity of words that the next time they sat down together at a kitchen table it would be for breakfast.

'Greg, I know this will sound foolish, but before we talk I'd like to call the Greys.'

He already knew her too well to have to ask why. 'Have you any kind of reasonable excuse for doing that?'

Julie nodded. 'A letter from Mrs. Grey this morning. She asked me to dinner there next week.' Tempted to tell him about the other letters, she decided not to. They were no more than part of the periphery of murder. She could tell him another time, if she still wanted to.

'Sit down. There are cigarettes in that box there,' she said, and began to leaf through the telephone book for a number she had not used before.

When she found it, she lowered herself on to the farther end of the couch on which Greg had seated himself, and dialled, thinking, I really am being a fool, but I can't help it. Of course Barbara is all right. Why shouldn't she be?

'May I speak to Mrs. Grey, please?'

'She isn't in, Miss Warner. She's out with Daddy.'

'Oh, it's you, Barby. I didn't recognize your voice, darling.'

'That's because I'm quite sick, probably. I mean that's probably why you didn't recognize my voice.'

Greg, who had been idly thinking what a pretty back Julie had, saw the sudden stiffening of that back, and switched his attention to what she was saying.

'I'm so sorry,' Julie said. 'I hope it's nothing serious.'

Sounding important as well as hoarse, Barbara replied, 'Not now. But it was a Strep Throat, and I was one hundred and four this afternoon before the doctor came with the sulpha tablets. Mummy says that for a little while I was Out Of My Head. I've never been Out Of My Head before.'

To Barbara, Julie's voice undoubtedly sounded quite natural. To Greg it did not. 'You aren't alone, are you, Barby?'

'Oh, no! Mummy never leaves me alone in the house. Though I don't see why not. Toni—that's my sister—is downstairs with her boy-friend. But she doesn't answer the phone when her boy-friend is here. I guess I don't blame her. I mean it wouldn't be very romantic if somebody was telling you how beautiful you are, and you answered, "Excuse me, but I have to answer the telephone".'

'No, I guess it wouldn't,' Julie said lightly. 'But you shouldn't be out of bed even if you have had sulpha.'

'I'm not. I'm in Mummy's bed until she gets back. I mean the phone is right beside me. And anyway, I'm nearly normal now. I guess the doctor is pretty good, even though I don't like him much. I wanted Dr. Markham, but Mummy said he wasn't for infections. I mean Dr. Markham is a surgeon, and Mummy said we had to have a—just a minute, and I'll get it—oh, yes, an internist. Mummy thinks Dr. Bartell is wonderful, but I don't think he should have talked to me about Susie. I mean especially he shouldn't have to me. He did it while Mummy was out of the room. I don't think that was very tactful do you, Miss Warner?'

'No I don't,' Julie replied, aware that Greg had moved so close to her that he was now hearing both sides of the conversation. 'But some people just don't think, Barby. I don't know Dr. Bartell, but I'm sure he just didn't think.'

There was a pause. Then Barbara said quietly, 'He was thinking, Miss Warner. That's why I don't like him.'

To maintain a light tone much longer was going to be difficult. 'Look, darling, you'd better not talk any more. Tell your Mummy that I got her very nice letter, and that I would love to have dinner with you. She can call me back tomorrow.'

'Not tomorrow!' Greg whispered, and she could feel the warmth of his breath on her cheek.

'Wait—I'll be busy tomorrow, Barby. Ask her to call on Sunday.'

'All right, Miss Warner. And I'm glad you're coming. I mean, that will be something to look forward to while I'm in bed. Good-bye for now.'

'Good-bye, Barby. Take very good care of yourself.'

Julie replaced the receiver, and turned slowly to Greg. 'You heard, didn't you? Barbara really is sick. Greg—I don't like it.'

To Greg, what he had just heard was so loathsome in its import, that the hard lines in his face were more revealing than he knew. 'I don't like it either,' he told her harshly.

'Tell me what you know. Everything you know. And what you plan to do about it,' Julie said evenly. 'I won't again behave as stupidly as I did tonight. I promise you. It was the ravine. Anything else, and I'll be all right.'

In spite of himself, the man's eyes went to the marks on her neck. The same pressure points. The same pattern of bruising which, though this time mercifully light, he had seen twice before. 'Have you any liniment in the house?'

'No. It's not bothering me, anyway.'

'It will later.'

'Then we'll do something about it later. Please, Greg, don't keep putting me off.'

His glance travelled around the long room, while he appreciated again what a pleasant place it was. Would she feel like living in it after tomorrow? He hoped she would, but she might not.

'My plan,' he began slowly, 'is both very simple and very complicated. The basic idea is simplicity itself. The complications lie in the fact that it will involve six people, none of whom, once the thing is set in motion, can afford to make a single mistake.'

'I am one of them?'

'You are one of them.'

'And the others?'

'Myself. One of Captain Velyan's men, Wingham for my choice. Clare Hurst. Her sister, Mrs. Wylie. Do you know Mrs. Wylie?'

Julie shook her head.

'You would like her. When this is all over you must meet her. You won't tomorrow, because what she has to do does not involve being here.'

Julie's eyes widened. 'Here?'

'Yes,' he told her soberly. 'Here. In this apartment. Can you face that part of it?'

'I can face anything but that damnable ravine.'

He understood this, and believed it, because to a lesser extent he felt as she did about the ravine. 'It will be daylight too. You'll find that makes a difference. By the way, how well do you know Clare?'

Julie considered the question. 'I think I know her better than I know most people, even though I haven't seen her very often. The thing that brought us together—the portrait—is the kind of thing that breaks down ordinary barriers.'

'Do you think she would be good under fire?'

'Yes,' Julie replied without hesitation. 'She is very like me in that respect. Continuing nervous strain could get her down. In a crisis there's nobody I would be more sure of.'

'My opinion, too. But I'm glad to have you under-write it.'

'And the sixth person?' Julie asked, even while she cried out silently against an answer she had already guessed.

Greg, his eyes never leaving her face, saw that she knew. 'Deborah.'

'Do you have to? Is there no other way?'

'None,' he told her flatly. 'If there were, I wouldn't do it, even though I think—but never mind about that now.'

'You've already talked to Clare?'

'Yes. She is more than prepared to go along with my idea. She, too, cares terribly about the Barbaras. Apart from that, she has almost too much confidence in myself for comfort.'

Julie leaned down to adjust the turn-ups of slacks which did not need adjusting, her bright hair hiding her face from him as she did so. 'Then we're alike in that respect, too. Clare and I.'

'Julie——'

She let her hand linger a moment in his, before with-drawing it and straightening up to look directly at him again. 'And the devil—who is he?'

Greg glanced at his watch. Then he lit two cigarettes, and gave one to her. 'We haven't much time left before Velyan gets here. The plan already talked over with Clare and Mrs. Wylie can be discussed when he arrives. Meanwhile, I will not only tell you who your devil is, but give you as clear an understanding of the man as I possibly can. And I must warn you that it will be a word picture, if anything, even more repulsive than the one you drew on paper.'

XVI

The table was medieval Italian, like everything else in the room, and had once belonged to the Medicis. On it, the front page of the *Courier* was an anachronistic blasphemy which consorted as ill with delicate wood inlay as it did with tapestried walls, a gilt-framed Florentine mirror, and the wrought-iron fretwork of a hanging light which had been fashioned for tallow candles.

The link, otherwise missing, between raw, twentieth century sensationalism, and the brooding opulence of a recreated Renaissance, was embodied in the man who leaned with feline grace against the table's edge.

In one white hand he held a crystal brandy glass. With the spatulate forefinger of the other he gently stroked cheap newsprint, each movement, soft as a caress, crossing and re-crossing the throat of the girl whose picture it featured. And as his eyes followed that motion, to and fro, to and fro, hypnotic in the evenness of a rhythm which did not vary, he felt again the warm texture of living flesh yielding to deliberate cruelty, and a tremor of pleasure ran through him like a flame.

There had been pleasure, too, in killing the dog, bare-handed and in darkness, but no lasting satisfaction. Even this blonde girl, her imagination peopled with devils, though young, was not young enough to provide a really satisfying memory which could be relived night after night until, at last growing dim, it must be replaced with a fresh one. And now, through the blundering idiocy of another man, he would have to kill her with none of the refinements to which she might have been subjected, and in broad daylight which precluded memories of any kind at all.

As he thought this, thwarted cruelty contorted his long, handsome face, scoring oblique furrows which ran sharply upwards from colourless eyebrows, hollowing the skin below cheekbones thrown into sudden ugly relief.

Yet, because the light from the iron chandelier failed to emphasize these things, when he raised his head to glare into the mirror he saw no conventional resemblance to the Devil, remained in ignorance of a truth he regarded as fantasy.

What he did see, however, were features too distinctively chiseled for present comfort. Enormously vain, he did not need to be convinced that they were memorable. And the four sketches, in the newspaper to which he returned his malignant gaze, were in themselves ample proof that a man could be thought to look like Satan while still looking, from certain points of view, like himself.

His finger never ceasing its regular, unhurried promise of injury yet to come, he thought, stupid little bitch, she will not be drawing any portraits tonight. Tonight she will have neither the strength nor the courage. By noon tomorrow she may have recovered sufficiently, but by noon tomorrow it will be too late. Whatever she has been persuaded to remember on paper, face to face she will no more know me from the devil than from Adam. And since all doors open to me, hers will be no exception. If I am seen going in? I heard a scream. I was too late. Who will doubt the word of Dr. Norman Bartell? Nobody.

Lifting his glass in a toast to his own abominable conceit, he was quite certain that, whatever the obstacles he might encounter, he would experience no difficulty in carrying out his aim. He was above suspicion.

He inhaled brandy which he savoured with a gourmet's conscious relish while he considered whether, in spite of handicaps, he might not still salvage some of the exquisite pleasure to be derived from inflicting pain.

XVII

An entire evening spent in the police station, was not, Tom Denning discovered, the most amusing way of passing time. Pained to find that he was unwelcome as a permanent fixture in Velyan's office, he wandered moodily between the desk sergeant, who refused to let him into the cell block without a pass, and the back room where two bored patrolmen took it in turns to go out and pick up drunks reported over the inter-com. Four drunks, brought in at different times during the evening, might have provided some entertainment, but, as it happened, did not.

By pure mischance he was in the back room when Wingham came in, and so missed seeing him by a margin which though small, was sufficient. And Sergeant Bell, who might have passed on this interesting item of information, chose to keep his own counsel. Not because he had been told to do so, but because the newspaperman had been getting on even his stolid nerves.

Denning's first intimation that events had moved at all was when, at a quarter to ten, he saw Velyan and Wingham coming down the corridor from the former's office.

Closing in on them with speed, he asked, 'What goes?'

'Nothing,' Velyan told him expressionlessly. 'I'm leaving now. You had better do the same thing.'

Angrily, Denning looked from one inscrutable face to the other. 'I wasn't born yesterday.'

'Lucky thing for your mother,' Wingham murmured.

Ignoring the detective completely, Denning addressed Velyan. 'I thought we were in this thing together?'

'I'm not responsible for what you think, Denning. And I define my own relations with the Press. When I have something for you, I'll let you know.'

Steady, Denning, steady, or your little red derrick will go in vain to this oil well in the future. You know Velyan well enough to know that if he's not talking, he's not talking. Period. Use your carrot-top instead of blowing it.

Moderating his tone, he said, 'All right, Captain. I'll be around in the morning.'

Undeceived by this capitulation, Velyan knew perfectly well that as soon as he walked out of the police station, Denning would first follow him, and then go to Julie Warner's. Since the two would add up to one and the same thing, he saw no harm in this.

Tom Denning, keeping a circumspect distance between his car and the police car, soon began to guess what direction it was headed. When his guess was confirmed, he saw at once how completely he had been out-manoeuvred.

'The double-dealing bastard,' he muttered, drawing up on the ravine side of the street opposite Julie's apartment. To wait was useless, he knew. Velyan would be no more ready to talk when he came out, than he had been when he went in. And if Julie's door had not been locked to him before, it would be now. Something had occurred. That much was only too obvious. It infuriated him that he could think of no way of finding out what had happened.

About to put his car into gear again, he instead turned off the ignition. Playing a hunch, he got out, crossed the street, and entered the alley which passed Julie's door and led to the back premises of the garage next door.

A little light filtered through from the street, but not much. However, there were very few cars behind the garage, and he located the station-wagon at once. He took a handful of matches from his pocket, and, striking one after another, examined the exterior of the car. There was no difficulty in seeing mud-splashed paint-work, wheels heavy with clay, and fresh scratches where chains had been fastened around the back bumper.

Only one place where you find clay like that around here, Denning, he told himself. Are you a man, or are you a rat? Both, undoubtedly, which makes your next move obvious.

That there had recently been an exceptional amount of traffic into the ravine was clear to him as soon as he manoeuvred his car around the first bend of the road which led down into it. At each curve the surface of the road was churned up; and skid marks which, again and again, drew his own wheels dangerously close to the forbidding palisade on either side, were undeniable evidence that at least three cars had gone that way not long before. One blue station-wagon, he reflected; one or more prowl cars; and one tow-truck. A story here which screamed to be printed. His own thoughts, however, as he negotiated the last part of the descent with extreme caution, were unprintable, revolving as they did around a police force which in his opinion had done him dirt.

Making no attempt to drive any further, he stopped the car, made sure it was on firm ground, and set out on foot along the path of light cast by his own headlamps.

Everywhere there were marks of fresh activity, already blurred by water which before morning would have sucked all trace of it back into a smooth, unrevealing coat of slime. Even the deeply gouged holes made by the rear wheels of the station-wagon were, when he reached them, more than half filled with a thick, evil-coloured liquid. Frowning, he studied those holes for several minutes, reconstructing a tantalizingly small fragment of what must have taken place. Then he switched his attention to the drier ground on the verge of the road. He was on the outer periphery of the light from his car when tenacity rather than luck rewarded him with a single, clear imprint of a dog's foot. Julie Warner had no dog. For that matter he had no proof that Julie herself had been in the ravine at all. This had been, in all probability, a police dog, and therefore trained to kill. With this realization, he felt the hair stir at the back of his neck, and became for the first time properly aware of the dark, menacing silence around him.

Tom Denning was not an imaginative man, but there were elements in that black silence which thoroughly unnerved him. The possibility that the dog might still be at large in the ravine was unpleasant enough in itself, but the brooding threat which made his skin crawl derived from no living source, and was therefore the more terrifying.

You're getting out of here, Denning, my boy, but fast, he decided. And he turned and hurried back to his car, the squelch of his feet, as the heavy clay dragged at them, emphasizing rather than dispelling a silence unlike any he had ever known before, or ever hoped to know again.

When he emerged from the ravine some ten minutes later, his normal sang-froid returned at once, and he wondered with irritation why the hell he had got the wind up as he had. But, as he drove home, his annoyance with himself was soon lost in renewed wrath against the police.

Nincompoops, the whole lot of them, he thought furiously as he let himself into the dreary hall of his boarding-house, and mounted the stairs to his unprepossessing room. Should have their badges ripped off them, the ineffectual peace-loving poops. They had really bungled something this time. And where did their unspeakable incompetence leave him? Out on a limb with no murderers, no corpses, and a panting populace who had been promised a portrait of the devil. That this was a promise he had known he was not going to fulfil had not mattered before. He had counted on producing in its stead an actual picture of an actual murderer, or one dead artist. Either would have done. Now it looked as if all he could count on was a sulphurous communication from the publisher followed by an interview which might result in an addition to the ranks of the unemployed. Mr. R. Wade Johnson—'just call me R.W.'—was scarcely literate in Denning's uncomplimentary opinion, but the *Courier* did not upset either its publisher or its public by using long words.

Muttering a few four-letter words which both owner and public would have understood readily enough, he kicked a battered armchair with less damage to the chair than to himself. In his mind's eye he saw a picture of Velyan with horns. From a bottom bureau drawer he took a bottle of whisky and poured a generous hooker into a heavy tumbler. Then he sat down on the edge of the bed and reviewed his position.

With what he had been able to find out this evening in spite of Velyan, he could filibuster, but no more. And to turn out a front page based on surmise would be to accomplish nothing beyond a king-size padlock on the police station with his name on it.

Denning, he told himself, somehow before noon to-morrow you've got to dig up some news that really is news in this town or you're a gone duck. Of course you could always do a nice piece on the weather, or the extension to the hospital....

Hazel eyes sharpened to pin-point attention, and he whistled softly under his breath. He set his glass down on the floor, pulled a clip of papers from his hip pocket, and selected two lined sheets covered with notes in his own private shorthand. The reporter he had assigned to cover the house where he had grazed a black Cadillac had already turned over irrefutable proof of what had previously been no more than unpleasant rumour. A good boy, Williams. He deserved a bonus. He might even get one if he could dig up anything in the morning related to tonight's fiasco. Meanwhile, Denning had in his hands a nice item for an inside page, but front page material only if he dared tie it up to the Cadillac's owner about whom he did not know nearly enough. Normally, he would have taken his time on this, but now he was in a spot, and knew it.

Williams had done a very thorough job considered the time at his disposal. No danger of libel. But plenty of danger of one T. Denning being run out of town on a rail for defaming an entire profession by playing up an unpalatable truth about a single member of that profession. One law for the Medes, and one for the Persians, he thought cynically. The way those pill-pushers stick together, no wonder they used to be called leeches. Three guesses what would happen to you, Denning, my boy, if you mosied up to the hospital with your rash of inquiries. Diagnosis—advanced case of Nosy Parker's disease. Treatment—the heave-ho.

'God-damn it,' he muttered, as he realized that the one person to whom he could have gone for a human being's reaction as well as a doctor's, was the one person at the moment least likely to co-operate with him. Under ordinary circumstances, Greg Markham would, he was sure, provide a fast fill-in on the man in whom he was interested: his personal reputation: the size and quality of his practice: and his standing in the hospital. In short, Greg would tell him whether the game would be worth the candle. It all depended really on how big a noise the man was. No matter how well justified the accusations which he, Denning, might level against this man, he would not be thanked for pulling a cornerstone out from under the hospital of which the town was so inordinately proud. All patients were peculiar about their doctors, were disinclined to believe ill of them even when given incontrovertible evidence of it. Ridiculous that one should be expected to place all medical men above suspicion, as if feet of clay went into purdah for good with the taking of an oath which had nothing to do with private foibles. And this, Denning thought with disgust, in the face of statistical evidence that the medical profession—apart from other deviations—boasted more murderers than any other given calling. If Caesar had had a harem, would all his wives have been above suspicion? Not bloody likely. None of which altered the hard fact that enough patients with enough money could be sufficiently peculiar, if they chose, to blow out his candle, for good.

With no idea that in his thinking he had brushed against a truth much more explosive than the one with which he was concerned, he ground a cigarette butt into a carpet which deserved no better treatment, and decided that there was nothing for it but to risk a black eye and tackle Greg at the hospital first thing in the morning.

XVIII

The grim young woman in black slacks and sweater who opened the door of the studio at five minutes past ten that evening, would have seemed almost plain to Velyan if he had not seen her before. The set, pale face, hard with a determination which subtly altered her whole appearance, warned him that to mention their last meeting, and its abortive results, would be a mistake.

'Come in, Captain Velyan. I'll take your coat.'

'Thank you, Miss Warner.'

'Greg, would you mix a drink for the Captain.'

He handed his coat to her, returned Greg's silent salute, and noted, in one apparently casual glance, a room which reflected taste and comfort. He saw paintings which made him wish this were merely a social call which would permit their closer examination: two doors on his right at the end of the room, one leading into the kitchen, and the other, as he surmised correctly, being that of the bathroom: on his left, beyond an empty easel, windows which must face west over the ravine: empty coffee cups and a full ashtray on a low table in front of a deep, chintz-covered couch on which two people had recently sat close together.

Oriented, in the time it took him to cross the room to a big chair beside the couch, he had also noted how at ease the surgeon was in this place. They were in tune, these two, each able to anticipate the wishes of the other without exchanging a word or a look. More than that, the delicate antennae of his own painfully acute sensitivity told him that at the moment they shared a common objective electric in its potentialities. Because he blamed himself so much for the near tragedy which had struck at this girl, he braced himself to refuse a further move involving anyone other than a police officer. That they should meet with him in this way, in quiet friendship untouched by reproach, was more than he had had any right to expect. And more than they were going to get.

'Ice, Captain?'

He looked up into unsmiling grey eyes, caught the same shadow of irony which he had heard in Greg's voice, and knew that his position was being challenged before he had stated it. 'Thank you,' he said without inflection.

'Captain Velyan,' Julie's voice was crisp and cool. 'You are undoubtedly preparing to tell Dr. Markham and myself, very politely, to mind our own business from now on. We sympathize with your point of view, but I wish to make it quite clear that we consider this even more our business than yours. And if you would with-hold any spoken judgement'—a slight softening of her mouth as she underlined the adjective took away any sting it might have had—'until you have heard what Dr. Markham has to say, it would save both time and possible embarrassment.'

Too acute, both of them, Velyan reflected. He should have made them come to him. Here, treated as a guest rather than a police officer, he had put himself at a disadvantage. He looked first at the girl, and then at the man, again seated on the couch, and his brief, sombre smile acknowledged their initial advantage and that together they were oddly formidable. 'Do I need to comment on that?'

'No,' Greg told him. 'Specific comments in regard to specific statements will be more useful in every way.

186

I will begin by telling you that I know—I'm not just guessing—I *know* who killed Susan Philips in the ravine last Tuesday night. And it is my absolute conviction that the same man attacked Deborah Hurst six months ago, under very similar circumstances. That he attacked Miss Warner tonight is, in my opinion, also a certainty.'

'The name of this man?'

The surgeon's eyes were grey steel as cold and pitiless as the rapier of his voice. 'Dr. Norman Bartell.'

One of Velyan's talents as a policeman was his ability to absorb shock without any change of expression whatsoever. 'That's a serious accusation, from every point of view, including your own, Dr. Markham.'

'I'm quite aware of that.'

'Then I suggest you substantiate it, if you can.'

'You're not inclined to believe me, Captain? I scarcely blame you.'

'I would prefer that you do the talking at present, Doctor.'

'My own preference, too,' Greg told him coolly. 'Julie would you bring down that drawing of yours, please.'

When she had done this, Greg placed it on the table near Velyan, and beside it a glossy page torn from a medical journal. 'Compare those two pictures with care, Captain, and give me an opinion.'

Velyan did as he was asked, and knew almost at once that what he saw before him—and he saw it quickly enough—was in itself of identity inconclusive as proof. However, taken in conjunction with the character of the man who presented it, it could not be brushed aside.

'There are points of similarity,' he said evenly.

'That's all you have to say?'

"At the moment, that is all I have to say.'

Julie spoke then, and Velyan marvelled at her self-possession.

'You're thinking,' she said, 'that he doesn't look like

the Devil, aren't you? Yet you see the similarity of nose and mouth, and you're wondering if, and how, he might. Look, if I rub out the Devil's dark eyebrows—like this— and eliminate the shadows under the cheek-bones—like this—and then sketch in the suggestion of straight, white eyebrows, you have, with no other change, a devil much less like the Devil but much more like himself. Haven't you'

Velyan stared at the quick magic which had drawn two pictures infinitely closer together than they had been. And, while refusing to be persuaded out of and, he nevertheless knew that he had unwillingly crossed an invisible boundary.

Julie pressed her advantage. 'Captain Velyan, did you ever as a child stand in the dark in front of a mirror and hold a flashlight under your chin? I can see that you did. What child hasn't. And don't you remember that it was no longer your face, but that of a terrifying stranger with eyes sunk in deep caverns, and jutting cheek-bones?'

With an effort Velyan tried to refuse a parallel which had real impact on his imagination.

'You make out a good case for a possibility, Miss Warner. Not a probability, however. And what you must bear in mind is that this present comparison has not, as any proper comparison should have, two sides. More plainly, you saw a distortion, but neither before nor afterwards did you see the original as it normally would have been. You saw only the Devil. You did not see the Devil and the man together.'

'And if she had?' Greg asked softly.

'If she had, I would naturally give your—shall we say—theory, more credence,' Velyan replied unemotionally. But even as he spoke, he read in both their faces a satisfaction which warned him that he had unwittingly committed himself.

'I'm glad to hear you say that.' Greg's manner was that of a man who has successfully won the first and most important lap of a race. A race the winning of which would give him so pleasure, but which had to be won at all costs. 'You will understand why I am glad, when I tell you that I, myself, have seen the distortion precisely as Miss Warner has portrayed it. But I, unlike Miss Warner, at the same time saw the man himself as he appears when he is not betrayed either by lighting or his own corruption.'

Convinced at lasty, Velyan saw a panorama running back across six months, the day by day infamy of which defied ordinary comprehension. How often has they passed one another on the street, the sidling, witless wreck of a young girl, and the sleek successful doctor? By the bedside of how many children had that slim, dark figure stood, and with what thoughts? How often had that figure, turned beast of prey, lurked in the darkness of the ravine, waiting...

That he now stood directly on the brink of the same awful understanding shared by Julie and Greg, was made starkly apparent by his next words. 'Who looked after Mrs. Philips when Susan died?'

'Bartell.'

'My God,' Velyan said, and for a moment Julie was excluded from a silence exchange which the two men could not have shared with any woman, even if they had wished.

It was Velyan who broke the silence, his calm voice according badly with the suffering of brilliant eyes which suffered for all humanity. 'Is there any more?'

'There's Barbara,' Julie said quietly.

Velyan had an excellent memory, and he knew the name of every child who had been in the station-wagon on the night of the murder. 'Barbara Grey? What about her?'

Julie's eyes appealed to Greg, and he told Velyan the gist of the telephone conversation Julie had had with Barbara earlier in the evening.

Velyan was no longer giving anything away. 'A transcript of what was said in that child's room might have helped. We haven't got such a transcript. As it stands, we have nothing, absolutely nothing we can work with at all.'

'You haven't?' Greg said pointedly.

'You think you have?'

'Let me put it this way. I hope I have.'

'What?'

When Greg replied, Velyan saw that he was again being forced into the anomalous position of friend as well as policeman. 'Nothing that it would profit you anything to know about in advance. And nothing that could be done by anyone other than myself. However, I need one man. Could you, without fanfare, put Wingham at my disposal from eight o'clock on tomorrow morning?'

'Wingham, or any of my men, for that matter, takes his orders from me and nobody else. I'm sorry, Markham, but that's flat. And although I can't stop either you or Miss Warner from making this your business if you insist on it, I must advise you that, however good your intentions, you'll be held responsible for any trouble you stir up.'

Unperturbed, Greg said, 'You're going to give Miss Warner police protection at present?'

'I am.'

'Is there any law that says it shouldn't be Wingham?'

Damn them both, Velyan thought violently. 'All right,' he said curtly. 'I'll assign Wingham.'

'And no other flatfeet in the vicinity? Above all, no tail on Bartell. It is of the utmost importance that he continue to think himself unsuspected in any way.'

Velyan fought a last and losing battle with himself. This was a competent, highly intelligent man with whom he was dealing, and a very determined one. With him Julie Warner would be safer than with any other. To refuse them what they asked would be not only to lose their confidence, but to impair his own ability to protect her. Too, there was always the possibility that they might accomplish what they had set out to do. In support of this was the fact that they had, between them, made an identification about which he had now no slightest doubt.

'All right,' he said. 'But on one condition. And that is that nobody goes into that damned ravine under any circumstances whatsoever.'

'Nobody will,' Greg told him decisively.

'Good. Where will Wingham contact you in the morning?'

'Ask him to meet me at Minelli's for breakfast, would you? It's the Italian restaurant on Carter Street. If I'm not there by eight o'clock, tell him to wait for me.'

Velyan emptied his glass and stood up. 'And tonight?' he asked, almost apologetically.

Greg hesitated before replying, not because he needed to search for his answer, but because the warm flush deepening in Julie's cheeks so much intrigued him. Then, having mercy on her, he said, 'Miss Warner has agreed to spend the night at the hospital.'

'The hospital!'

'I know. At first glance it may not seem the wisest place, but for that very reason it is. Take my word for it. He will foul his own nest only as a last resort. No, the hospital is the best solution in every way. Miss Warner found the only other possibility, shall we say—unsuitable.'

'Greg, really! You might make it a little clearer that your so-called other possibility was quite impossible!'

Velyan regarded the two who now stood beside him as he put on his coat, and thought it not at all impossible. He had the grace not to say so. 'You'll be at the hospital yourself, of course, Markham?'

'Yes. I've already booked a room for Miss Warner opposite my office. I'll spend the night in the office.'

'Where,' Julie said, 'I have been given to understand there is a very uncomfortable couch.'

'Not a kind girl but a nice girl,' Greg murmured.

Velyan was surprised to find himself smiling. God

preserve them both, he thought. And then because he had a superstition that to wish anyone good luck verbally was to invoke the opposite, he simply said, 'Good night.'

When he had gone, Greg said very quietly, 'Julie— will you wish me luck?'

Julie's eyes told him that she would now find it difficult to deny anything he asked of her. And when he kissed her for what was only the second time, she felt as if her very bones were melting.

Finally releasing her, he said, 'Go and change now. And go quickly.'

He turned his back, and heard her collecting clothes from the cupboard and afterwards shutting the bathroom door.

For a few minutes he studied the studio as he had not studied it before, assessing distances and the place of the furniture. The couch, which was against the wall directly opposite the door from the stairs, would do very well where it was. The coffee table would have to be got out of the way. And the large chair, which obstructed a direct passage from the kitchen, must be moved to the end of the room near the windows. Without wasting time, he did these things, and, regarding the result, decided that it was an arrangement which looked natural enough.

He then went into the kitchen and redistributed the furniture there. When he had done this, there was a clear space just inside the doorway but well out of sight of anyone near to, or leaning over the couch in the main room.

He looked into the stove, checked the overhead grill, and then opened the freezer compartment of the refrigerator. Relieved to find several kinds of meat, he selected a steak with a good edging of fat, and laid it out on the table to thaw. It would have been a nuisance to have had to stop at a butcher's in the morning. If I were a good cook, he reflected, I wouldn't know as well as I do what a hell of an odour burning steak can produce.

Now, merely putting in time, he found himself irresistibly drawn towards the stack of canvases in the far corner of the studio. Handling them with great care, he put them aside one by one until he came to the vivid, laughing portrait of Deborah as he had never really known her.

Gazing at it, seeing the mischief in the sparkling brown eyes, and the sweet curve of the mouth, he thought he had never seen a lovelier young girl, nor one that it would have been harder for a mother to lose. In his imagination he could see her running gracefully up the walk to a white bungalow, hear her merry voice call out as she scattered school-books in the small hall. Could see her go at once in search of Clare, who must have looked—and could again, so much like her. Could see them laughing together over the small, unimportant happenings of a day which between them they made important.

God willing, he told himself. God willing....

XIX

Mrs. Wylie was in the habit of arriving at the hospital a few minutes before nine in order to take over the main desk at nine exactly. On that Saturday morning, however, she came through the revolving doors before it was fully light. When she knocked at the partially open door of Greg's office on the third floor it was no later than seven-thirty.

He answered her knock at once, and his smile was particularly warm. 'Come in. You're very prompt.'

Small lines, not usually very noticeable, were in evidence around Mrs. Wylie's eyes. 'I didn't need an alarm clock.'

'Raining out?'

'No. But I think there will be a storm later.'

'You spent the night at your sister's?'

'Yes.'

'Everything under control there?'

Unconsciously Mrs. Wylie put up her hand to assure herself that her cap of white curls was as neat as usual. 'If you mean Clare, yes. You know, Dr. Markham, she defeats me. She is more like her real self this morning than she has been for six months.'

Greg nodded. It was what he had hoped for. 'And yourself?'

'I'll be all right,' Mrs. Wylie told him briefly. 'Is Miss Warner awake yet?'

'Not as far as I know. But I'm leaving now, and I want you to sit here,' he indicated the chair behind the desk, 'and keep your eyes on that door across the hall. She is not to come out, and nobody is to go in.'

'If she wants some breakfast?'

Greg considered this for a moment. 'No. She'll have to wait until I get back, which will be no later than a quarter to nine. I haven't booked her in formally. If anyone asks questions, she is a private patient of mine in for observation, and you don't know her name.'

'And if someone wants to know what I'm doing here?'

'Tell them you're helping me with over-due accounts. If you really want to act the part, you'll find a list in the top right-hand drawer of those who find it easier to be opened up themselves than to open their cheque-books.'

Mrs. Wylie hesitated, and then said, 'Where will you be—if I need to get in touch with you?'

'You won't,' he assured her. 'But just for the record, I'll be at Minelli's. I'm meeting Captain Velyan's man there.'

Again Mrs. Wylie hesitated, before asking, 'And Miss Warner? Is she——'

'She's like Clare,' he told her soberly. 'She can, and does, rise to an occasion.'

That they had neither of them mentioned Deborah was a hiatus of which they were both acutely aware. Deborah, the most important cog in the precise mechanism of a plan which, to be successful, must run as smoothly as a Swiss watch, was as ignorant of this as she appeared to be of nearly everything else.

'I must go now,' Greg said. 'The fort is yours.'

Grimly preoccupied, he almost ran into Tom Denning in the deserted main lobby, before he saw him at all.

'You in a hurry, chum?'

The surgeon looked up sharply, and his face darkened with anger. 'If I had met you anywhere but here, those would have been the last words you uttered for twenty-four hours. Now, get out of my way, and stay out of it.'

Denning, assuming his most winning expression, congratulated himself for having chosen this spot and been on it so early. 'Is that any way to speak to an old friend?'

Greg felt his hands knotting into fists. 'As of yesterday you are no friend of mine. If your hide wasn't as thick as your crust, you would have known that without being told.'

Apparently genuinely injured, Denning allowed his face to convey this sense of injury, while verbally coming to the point without further loss of time. 'Look, Greg, you've got a character around here called Bartell, and I——'

To his complete amazement, the surgeon took him by the elbow, swung him firmly but not urgently in the direction of the side entrance, and said, 'We'll talk about whatever you have on your mind on our way downtown.'

Of all the accursed luck, Greg thought, swearing silently, this is the limit. He can't know, or even suspect the truth. And yet he's got on to something that has started him sniffing in the right direction at the worst possible moment. How little can I tell him, and still head him off?

'Whoa back, pal! Not so fast. I have my own crate here.'

Greg's voice warned against argument. 'I have business to attend to, and no time to waste. You talk to me in my car or not at all.'

The change of pace, in all ways, had been so sudden, that Tom Denning had had no opportunity to conjecture about the reason for it. One thing was clear though. The name Bartell had been his open-sesame. This was good enough to go on with. More than good enough, since it appeared that any danger of assault and battery had passed.

'Okay, Doctor. Where you go, I go. Your car shall be my car.' He glanced at a hard profile out of the corner of his eye, as he added insinuatingly, 'And your secrets shall be my secrets?'

Greg unlocked his car, got in, and when Denning was seated beside him, said curtly, 'What do you want to know about Bartell, and why?'

Succinctly, Denning told him, finishing with, 'What I need to know is, do I go ahead with this, or is it another hypocritic skeleton for the Hippocratic closet?'

Driving automatically, Greg knew that under ordinary circumstances he would have advised Denning, for his own sake, to steer clear of scandal in connection with so prominent and well-connected a man, and one who numbered among his patients fully half of the governing board of the hospital. Himself convinced that a doctor's morals should be above reproach, he would then have been glad enough to see this advice disregarded. Now, however, he needed some real assurance that Tom Denning would back down, would stay clear of an arena no less dangerous than the arenas of ancient Rome.

He knew he was taking too long to answer Denning's question, and that his abrupt volte-face had aroused a curiosity which would not be satisfied with any casual, evasive explanation. His own actions had laid a stress on Bartell's name which could not be lightly dismissed. But with every block he put between himself and a locked room on the third floor of the hospital, a rising anxiety made it increasingly difficult to concentrate on a problem thrown at him with so little warning. From this distance, Mrs. Wylie seemed too frail a defence to have left between Julie and a threat which might have begun to move towards her.

Denning's hopeful voice prodded him. 'Borderline case? Not too many moneybags in the background?'

To clutch at this straw would be to have the whole staff of the *Courier* all over town in less than an hour, weighing its pros and cons. 'No. There's a "Keep Out" notice on that lawn as big as a highway sign from your point of view.'

'Then what's the catch, chum? And don't waste breath telling me there isn't one.'

As they turned into the court-square square, Greg heard the low growl of thunder in the west. A vibration, diffused by thin, grey fog, which seemed to emanate not from the solid clouds above but from the windless depths of the ravine.

The offices of the *Courier* were just ahead. It was as far as he intended that Denning go with him. He braked, and came to a stop between a milk truck and a child's bicycle, and even as he did so, he recognized the only possible course open to him. A course so bold in its simplicity that it could not fail. He would tell Denning the exact truth, but Denning, sharp though he was, would not realize what that truth implied.

He was a poor liar. If he had attempted a lie he could not have looked at the reporter and made it stick. Now, he turned and faced him directly.

'Look, Tom,' he said, 'chance and your own long nose have led you into the middle of something bigger than you have so far guessed. Unofficially, a charge has been laid against Dr. Bartell infinitely more serious than the one you've made. At the moment, however, it's touch and go whether that charge can be substantiated. By noon today I'll be in a position to tell you whether it can or not. I think it can. And if so, it will make a big story for you. Exclusive. But if one whisper of *any kind* gets through to him now, he'll cover his tracks, and that will be that until he slips again, if he ever does.'

Denning who spent his life sifting truth from false-hood, knew truth when he heard it. His busy mind ran over a host of possibilities, any or all of which would please him extremely. 'You won't drop a hint, Greg? Unfortunate patient Passes On under suspicious circumstances? Celebrated doctor, too fresh from illegal pleasures, mixes prescriptions? Death certificate which won't bear to close inspection?'

With cold satisfaction, Greg knew that he had done precisely the right thing. 'I can tell you nothing now. But you have my promise that before one o'clock I will call you and give you the complete story, win or lose, to do what you like with. In return I want your promise to stay out of this completely until you hear from me.'

It was not everyone who would accept Tom Denning's promise as worth having, a state of affairs which was a deep, personal affront to him. Unable to see himself as others saw him, heartless and unscrupulous to a degree, he considered his word as good as anyone's. That this man, for whom he had a marked respect, should be prepared to accept his word, was a psychological lever whose strength Greg himself did not fully appreciate. From a practical point of view, he felt that, given the kind of lead he expected, the *Courier* unhampered by medical ethics, could establish proof of guilt on its own if need be.

'It's a deal,' he said. 'And here, fair sir, is my hand upon it.' With which he shook hands with himself.

Against his will, Greg felt his personal anger cooling. 'All right. You'll hear from me. Now this is where you get off.'

Without remonstrance, Denning stepped out on to the sidewalk. Before closing the door, he put his head in, and said, 'With a view to our future relations, you might bear it in mind that it was Miss Warner who came to me, and not the other way 'round.'

'That was her mistake.'

'Just what I was trying to point out,' Denning said gently. 'Her mistake. Not mine.'

For a moment Greg watched the loosely-knit figure saunter towards the shabby entrance of the newspaper offices, and accepted the fact that if there were to be a future for Julie and himself, that future would see the three of them sitting some evening in a downtown bar in perfect amity.

Then, looking across at the clock in the church tower, seeing that it was almost eight o'clock, he pulled out into a ragged stream of early morning traffic, hearing as he did so another deep rumble of thunder.

XX

I'm not really thinking at all, Clare told herself, as she helped Deborah into a green raincoat now almost too small for her. It's as if I were two people. One who follows a script so well memorized that error is out of the question. And another who watches, physically set apart, praying to her God as she has never prayed before.

'There you are, darling. We're going to Miss Warner's. But I told you that, didn't I?'

Submissive, her head canted at its own curious angle, Deborah stood beside the front door without replying. Nothing in her blank face showed that she had heard, much less understood, what had been said to her.

Clare, who might, in six months, have become accustomed to conversations never anything other than one-sided, and yet who had not, forced herself to go on with chatter as meaningless to herself as it appeared to be to her daughter.

'Let's see, where did I put my umbrella? Right in the back of the cupboard as usual. Wasn't that silly of me? You'd think with all this horrible weather I'd be bright enough to leave it beside the door, wouldn't you? Now, I think we're all ready. You like going to Miss Warner's, don't you, darling? Well, it's nice for me to come with you today.'

She checked the latch on the door, took a slack young hand in her own thin one, and set out by Deborah's own torturous route for Julie's apartment.

There had been a time when to walk with Deborah was a rhythmic pleasure, their steps matching perfectly. Now it was a jerky, irregular failure to coincide against which Clare must steel herself afresh each time they left the house together.

'There's going to be a storm, I think. You always used to like storms.' She upbraided herself for the past tense which would creep in no matter how carefully she guarded against it. 'You enjoy storms, don't you, darling. Just like me.'

A wire-haired terrier came running from a front porch to frisk at their heels, barking excitedly, but to Deborah he might not have been there at all. Without any alteration in her uneven, sideways gait, she continued to move forward at Clare's side, the slight shuffle of her shoes like an echo from the dead leaves rustling in the gutter.

Clare nodded an occasional greeting to people who, if she had been alone, would have spoken to her. For once she failed to resent cowardice of which she would not have been guilty had the positions been reversed. All she cared about on this sullen Saturday morning was reaching her objective undetained, unmolested in any way. Already, ahead of her, she could see the back windows of Julie's apartment, and the lane leading into the parking space behind the garage.

As they walked up the lane, and cut across the parking lot at a diagonal, Deborah's head twisted further and further around until her chin was almost resting on her shoulder. And in the alley itself, when they reached it, Clare saw, as she had known she would, that the girl's eyes were closed, and that she guided herself along the brick wall with her hand.

Her chest constricted with actual pain, Clare thought, that she should come here at all is the ultimate proof of her trust in Julie—and in me. And I bring her here perhaps to shatter what small trust in the world is left to her.

She looked at her watch as they went up the stairs, and saw that it was just twenty past nine. With all her heart she hoped that they had not arrived ahead of Julie and Greg. Her courage had carried her this far alone, but now she needed their support, and needed it badly. To wait on a badly lit landing, listening to her own voice phrasing the aimless nonsense which passed for conversation with this poor, brutally misused child of hers, would be more than she could stand.

And when Deborah's overlong nails scraped against the door panel as she herself raised her hand to knock, she almost cried aloud.

Julie's husky voice seemed to Clare the most beautiful sound she had ever heard. 'Hello, Clare—Deborah. Come in. Dr. Markham is here too. Isn't this nice.'

Clare, looking at Julie as she took off her own coat and Deborah's, knew that only another woman would see through skillful make-up to strain she would not have noticed if she had not been looking for it. She hoped that she had done even half as good a job on herself.

'There you are, Debbie,' she said. 'Now find yourself somewhere to sit down.'

Julie smiled. 'I think I might start to work on Deborah's picture right away, don't you, Clare?'

'That might be a good idea.'

'And I,' said Greg, in his turn smiling into a witless, unresponsive countenance, 'am going to watch the artist at work.'

'Cigarette, Clare? Greg?' Julie, in a white blouse with a high collar which hid the base of her throat, seemed so much as ease that for an instant Clare wondered if she had dreamed it all. The careful step by step planning which had led to this moment. The detailed, precise instructions which each of them had received from the tall man now casually lighting a cigarette as if he had nothing more important on his mind. He insisted on this casualness in advance because none of them could know how much Deborah might or might not understand if they talked at all freely.

'Thank you,' Clare said, and saw that both his hand and her own were steady as he lighted a cigarette for her.

Even where they were to sit during this time of waiting, which would be harder on them in some ways than what was to follow, had been arranged ahead of time.

'Let's see now,' Greg said. 'Would this be the model's stand?'

'That's right,' Julie told him.

He lifted a straight, low-backed chair away from the wall, and set it down in the middle of the room facing the north window. 'That about right?'

'A little bit further forward,' Julie suggested. 'There, that's more the way we usually have it, isn't it, Debbie?'

Clare, already seated on the couch, thought, they are incredible, both of them. They set their scene as if there were chalk marks to guide them, and make it seem as if it were just happening that way. Doing her own part, she assured herself that the portrait Julie was putting on the easel could not possibly be seen from where she was. They had decided that, although Deborah had never shown the slightest interest in what lay on the other side of a canvas whose blank side she seemed content to look at for hours, it would be taking chances to use anything other than the only portrait of her which now remained. And also as usual, to put the canvas in place after Deborah had taken up the position to which she had grown used.

'Where will the audience bother you least, Julie?' Greg asked.

'Oh, I don't know. I don't think it matters much. We won't be paying any attention to them, anyway, will we, Debbie?'

'Then I think this looks comfortable,' Greg remarked, and settled himself quietly in a chair almost directly behind Deborah. Clare, feeling the constriction in her throat again, saw his hand go to his pocket and had a fleeting glimpse of a small bottle and a square pad of gauze before they were put down behind a stack of magazines on the small table beside him.

Clare lit a cigarette from one less than half smoked, and saw that Julie, brush in hand, her expression absorbed, untroubled, was already at work. Is she really working, Clare wondered, and decided that she probably was, because she herself would have given a great deal to have had something with which to occupy herself. Thrown back on her own thoughts, she asked herself desperately is she could conceivably make a mistake. If something were to go wrong—really wrong, would she ever be able to forgive herself?

In the silence, the ticking of a clock which she could not see was like slow hammer strokes, and she wished frantically that they had not decided it would be better in this interval not to talk. Is this waiting as hard on Beryl, she wondered. And knew that it must be, if only because Beryl, at her desk in a black and white tiled lobby was, in any way that counted, alone with what she had to do.

Mrs. Wylie, unlike her sister Clare, hated storms. The muffled, increasingly frequent reverberations of thunder, which seemed to swell up out of the ravine beyond the revolving doors, were successive assaults on her nervous system. And the visibly jerking hands of the electric clock above the doors actually seemed to flick against her each time they moved. Five minutes—four minutes—three minutes to ten.

Would he come in as usual at ten o'clock? Would he come precisely at ten, as he always did? And if he didn't, how long could she continue to keep her telephone receiver off the hook without one of the switchboard girls coming over to tell her it was off? And if someone else came up to the desk at the same time he did, could she still do what she had to do?

Two minutes… one minute….

On the periphery of her field of vision she saw the door of the side entrance opening. Simultaneously the receiver of the telephone was in her hand, and she was apparently deep in the middle of a conversation, her own side of which was unusually distinct.

'I'm sorry, Miss Warner, I can't quite catch what you're saying. Dr. Markham? Yes, he's in the hospital, but I'm afraid he's operating just now. What was that? Can you speak a little more clearly, Miss Warner? Yes, I'll do my best. Yes. Good-bye.'

Although she had not heard him come, every nerve in her small body told her the exact instant when he had reached the desk.

'Something the matter, Mrs. Wylie?'

There was no acting about a start she could not re-press. 'Dr. Bartell! I didn't know you were there.'

His deep-set eyes intent on her, he said softly, 'You seemed to be having some trouble.'

'No,' Mrs. Wylie said. Then, seeming to change her mind, she said, 'Well, a little, perhaps. One of Dr. Markham's patients wants to see him urgently, and he isn't available at present.'

The deep-set eyes shifted their focus to a call-board which showed an illuminated arrow beside the name of Dr. Gregory Markham. The proof that even this small detail, insisted on by the surgeon, had been of real importance, helped to fortify Mrs. Wylie. 'The connection was very bad,' she went on evenly. 'Probably due to the

206

storm. I couldn't hear everything that was said. But she sounded very upset.'

'She?' The single word was a quiet hiss.

'It was a Miss Warner. I believe she had some kind of accident last night. Possibly she's suffering from reaction now. But I really don't know what she said. I think, since Dr. Markham won't be free for some time, that I had better see if someone else could go out there. What do you think, Doctor?'

The long, suave face betrayed nothing. The suave voice said, 'Perhaps it would be a good idea if I myself went out and saw—Miss Warner, did you say?'

'Yes, Doctor. But aren't you——'

'Too busy? As long as it is somebody who needs a doctor—then that is my business. Have you her address?'

I know her address, and you know it, Mrs. Wylie thought grimly, even as she said, 'No, Doctor. Just a minute while I look it up. Dr. Markham will be very grateful to you, I know. He has, well, rather a special interest in this particular patient.'

She leafed through the telephone directory, her hands ice-cold, while she saw clearly that it could have happened just like this. It was, on the surface of it, so natural, so ordinary, that on both sides it would have been almost difficult to say the wrong thing.

'Here it is,' she said. 'Ravine Street, number 107A. Shall I make a note of it for you, Doctor?'

Without any appearance of haste, he was already moving away from the desk. 'No, thank you, Mrs. Wylie. I can remember it.'

With as little appearance of haste, Mrs. Wylie picked up her telephone again, pressed the red button which would give her an outside line, and dialled a number. The first ring brought a response, and with Clare's low voice in her ear, Mrs. Wylie found that she was trembling uncontrollably. It was a terrible effort to speak distinctly. 'Mr. Jones? I have the report on your wife, and——'

The only one, of the four in the studio, who did not make some involuntary move when the telephone rang, was Deborah.

Julie's voice was not quite even. 'You take it, will you, Clare?'

Clare, ahead of her cue, was already crossing the room. 'Hello?'

'Mr. Jones, I have the report——'

'Miss Warner is busy just now,' Clare said steadily, but she had already put down the receiver by the time she started saying it.

Julie, her paint-brush making ineffectual smears on the edge of her canvas, knowing that in thirty seconds she was going to see something which would seem monstrous no matter how she rationalized it, said, 'Clare, would you put on some coffee?'

With one agonized look at Deborah, Clare turned and fled to the kitchen.

Simultaneously, Greg, his face a granite mask, rose from his chair, and with a single, noiseless stride was behind Deborah. With one arm he pinioned both of hers to her sides, while with the other he forced her head backwards, a square pad of cotton tight across her nose and mouth.

Julie's brush fell from fingers which refused to hold it. She saw the girl's eyes widen and roll in wild animal terror. Saw her back arch like a bow against constraint from which she could not break free. Saw her heels drumming against the floor in terrible, spasmodic frenzy.

Clare, hearing that frantic tattoo, clutched the edge of the sink and fought back a wave of nausea. Then she opened the oven, and slid a steak pan close against an electric grill which was already red-hot. By the time she had closed the oven, she could no longer hear any sound from the other room.

'All right, Julie,' Greg said quietly.

It was harder for him than it was for me, Julie told herself. It was hell for him, but he didn't have to watch her face. Yet when she saw him lift the limp girl in his arms, and lay her with infinite tenderness and care on the couch, she knew that he had not needed to see her face.

'Not much time, Julie.'

Snapped out of immobility by the authority in his voice, Julie went to the west window and pulled back curtains always drawn when Deborah was in the apartment. Then she went to the couch, aware here of the sickly sweet smell of chloroform, and turned on a lamp which drove the grey light back into the corners of the room, and brought a sheen to Clare's dark head bent now over her child as she washed the wan, blank face with quick, gentle confidence.

Julie raised her eyes, saw that Greg had left the room, and knew that he was signalling to Wingham from the kitchen window. A current of air brought the acrid smell of burning meat into the studio. A smell not yet strong enough to dispel entirely the odour of chloroform, but already sufficient to make it less readily identifiable.

She looked down again, and saw Clare touch the waxen cheeks and dark curls with perfume.

A minute later, Wingham, wearing neither hat nor overcoat, came in, and without a word, passed swiftly through the room. Julie, who had expected him to say something, knew that he had not done so in order to make it easier for Clare and herself to ignore his presence as they must do. And when she gathered up the towel and wash-cloth which Clare had used, and took them into the bathroom, she did not even glance at him where he stood pressed against the wall just inside a door which she left, partially open, exactly as she had found it.

A billow of smoke from the kitchen told her that Greg had opened the oven door briefly, and would now have turned the oven off. The damp air from the open kitchen window would very quickly clear the kitchen itself of smoke which otherwise might have made him cough as she herself was now doing. There is nothing he hasn't anticipated, she thought soberly. God grant that Clare and I don't let him down.

She blinked eyes which stung, and her gaze locked with Clare's, to see a reflection of her own thought as clearly as if it had been spoken.

Slowly Clare backed away from the couch until she was out of the direct line between it and the front door.

Julie stayed where she was, close to the door, listening for the first sound on the stairs. And it was as if the two men, one hidden in the kitchen, the other in the bathroom, had ceased to exist. They were alone now, she and Clare, in a smoky silence broken only by the heavy breathing of the motionless figure on the couch. Alone, waiting for potential death already on its way towards them. What they were to do say, when death actually came into the room with them, had been rehearsed up to a certain point only. After that they must depend on their wits, must ad lib without error.

Four minutes—five minutes—how long to wait, Julie wondered with cold calm. Greg had timed it at fourteen minutes from the hospital to the studio through the comparatively light traffic of mid-morning. He had been both anaesthetist and surgeon on the night when Deborah had been brought up out of the ravine. He knew what her tolerance to chloroform had been then. Would it have changed? Would Deborah start struggling back to consciousness too soon? Or, as was more likely, because he had wanted to take no chance of this, would she, Julie, have to stall with death longer than was possible? Death, if it struck, could not strike in three directions at once. Towards which of them would it turn first—Clare, Deborah, or herself? Deborah was already helpless. It would not be Deborah. Clare had not had the temerity to point the finger at death. It would not be Clare. It would, as she had known all along, be herself.

This bright, quiet room is a jungle, she thought with-out emotion. And we are hunters who wait beside a fresh kill for the tiger; listening for a stealthy footfall; hoping that a broken twig will warn us; knowing that he is already close, poised to spring—to kill again.

Was that a stair-tread creaking? No—yes!

She jerked the door open, and saw a dark figure already halfway up the stairs.

'Dr. Markham?' Her hand felt as if it were welded for all time to the door-knob.

The dark figure seemed to materialize rather than arrive on the step below the landing, blocked from coming any further by her own body.

'No. Dr. Markham was unable to come, Miss Warner. I came instead.' The voice was deep, soothing, threatened to mesmerize her as did the glittering eyes beneath colourless eyebrows. 'I am Dr. Bartell.'

I don't really recognize him, Julie thought blankly. But I know him because he is evil incarnate. 'Oh—Doctor, how good of you. I mean I did need a doctor so badly.' I sound like a hysterical fool. And that is good. Oh, God, let Clare's signal come quickly, quickly. 'I didn't know what to do, Doctor, and I was quite frightened. I mean, it was so unexpected.'

The voice humoured her even while it exerted pressure on her. 'Now, now, Miss Warner, everything will be all right, I assure you. If you'll just step back, we'll go inside where I can look after you.'

Julie did not move. 'I'm afraid I haven't made myself clear. It was such a bad connection when I called the hospital. I felt that the woman there wasn't hearing me.

Or perhaps she isn't very bright. I——'

'Please, Miss Warner. You are over-excited. Perhaps you don't realize that we are still standing in your doorway. I can do nothing here, my dear young lady.'

Not even kill me with as much safety as you would like, or as much deliberation. Because I know now that is the way you want it with me, too. Clare—Greg—for God's sake, I can't go on much longer. 'Oh, how stupid of me,' she said, and there was a small catch in her voice. 'I didn't realize I was quite so upset. Of course, we must——'

Like a bird fascinated by a snake, she found herself tongue-tied, moving backwards against her will as he stepped up on to the landing, not a tall figure, but one which suddenly seemed to tower over her.

Clare's slight cough, almost lost in thunder now rolling directly overhead, brought him up short.

'There's someone with you!'

'Yes, of course,' Julie babbled. 'That's what I've been trying to tell you, Doctor. That's why I need you. I mean, I'm all right, but she suddenly had this sort of fit, and fainted, and I was terrified.'

Bracing herself, she now did the hardest thing of all. She put her hand on his arm, repulsion running through her like a poison, and pulled him with her into the room and across to the couch.

His self-possession in the face of what must have been an incalculable shock, was beyond belief. The flat lips flattened a trifle more, but that was all.

Clare stepped forward, her tone a perfect mixture of helpless concern and apprehension. 'Please do something, Doctor. It's my daughter. And neither Miss Warner nor I have been able to do anything to help her. We were just talking after having put something in the oven for lunch, when she—she fell down. I hope it was the right thing to lift her up?'

If he had needed it, Clare had given him time to collect himself, to decide to do nothing other than behave as a doctor would when called in to see a patient; or to kill all three of them.

Julie clenched teeth which threatened to chatter audibly, and waited for him to make the move that would either blast their hopes completely, or give them whatever chance of success they had ever had. Would he go through at least the first motions of examining Deborah, or would he turn on her, Julie, without further delay?

When he put down the black bag he was carrying, and leaned over the girl, Julie's jaws were locked so tightly together she was, for the time being, physically as dumb as Deborah.

Deborah who, opening brown eyes to stare straight into the face no more than inches from her own, was suddenly screaming as she might have screamed on a vivisectionist's table.

With a single bound, a man, whose expression was that of the Devil incarnate, placed himself against the further wall. For a fraction of a second he crouched there, malignant eyes flickering between Julie and Clare, before leaping towards Julie. With a shuddering impact he crashed into the tall man who hurled himself across the room to intercept that leap. Snarling and spitting, fighting with insane fury, he was borne to the floor beneath the combined weight of two men whose avenging fury more than matched his own. Between them they pinned him down and tied him hand and foot. In a matter of minutes they had him ungently trussed and out of the room.

Julie, though afterwards able to recall all this, was at the time aware of nothing but Clare shielding Deborah from any sight of it while she talked quickly, soothingly, her thin face so illumined with joy it seemed to shed a light of its own.

Why, she's beautiful, Julie thought.

The last rough echo of sound died away in the stair-well, and Julie felt tears on her cheeks as she heard a voice she had never heard before. A clear, girl's voice that matched in clarity the brown eyes, anxious but trusting, which were fixed on Clare to the exclusion of anything else.

'Mummy—what happened? Oh, Mummy, I've had the most horrible, horrible dream. I can't tell you!'

'Don't try, Debbie darling. Horrible dreams are best forgotten as quickly as possible.'

'At first I thought it must have been real. But if it had been—I would be hurt. And I'm not. Not at all.'

'Sometimes,' Clare said gently, 'it's hard to tell what is real and what isn't. Sometimes one has to decide that for oneself, darling.'

Julie turned away and stumbled towards the door, making no effort to check her tears. She wasn't needed any more. Clare was more than capable of handling her miracle by herself.

Greg, when he came back up the stairs ten minutes later, found her sitting in semi-darkness on the top step, crying as though she would never stop.

Quietly he sat down beside her, and held her to him.

Her voice muffled by sobs, Julie said, 'You did it. She's come back. Greg—you did it! She's come all the way back.'

'We did it, darling.'

'Greg, believe me, I practically never cry,' Julie said. And cried harder than ever.

* * *

On the second Tuesday of December of that year, two things, which were generally remarked on, happened in the town.

In the morning a final sentence of criminal insanity was passed.

214

In the afternoon the first snow began to fall, clean, white, and beneficent, gently covering the acres of raw stumps which were all that remained of the ravine.

Tom Denning, his feet on his desk, leaned back, whistling softly under his breath, as he listened to the most musical sound he knew.

'Read all about it!' 'Read all about it!'

He had not, he reflected, been such a fool after all in attaching himself to an afternoon paper. Two unrivalled, magnificent scoops in the space of less than a month. Not bad, Denning, my boy. Not bad at all. But now what?

His whistle fading into silence, he looked morosely at a tentative lay-out for the following day when his 'Build the Most Beautiful Playground in America' campaign would be launched.

How nauseatingly dull, he thought. And to think that you should have wittingly helped to bring yourself to this, my boy, that you should have been sucker enough to have boiled your own golden egg. Is there anything at all that you can still salvage from this unhappy debacle? Do you dare, ten days from now, Denning, to run a wedding picture surrounded by Devils?

Sighing audibly, he knew that he dared not.

Véhicule Press